Praise for Brenda Williamson's
A Beautiful Surrender

"What a phenomenal book!...The plot is extraordinary, and the characters are astonishing....some of the strongest characters I have read; the Princess Katerina, as well as "Duke" Dax, are both typically leadership material. While Dax was led to believe that Katerina was a snob, the characteristics of her were definitely those of a strong, caring lady. Dax was quickly smitten but knew of no way to abort Talbot's scheming...This is the most remarkable book I have read in a long time... To say this book is award winning will still not do justice to this marvelous work!"

~ *Brenda Talley, The Romance Studio*

A Beautiful Surrender

Brenda Williamson

A Samhain Publishing, Ltd. publication.

Samhain Publishing, Ltd.
512 Forest Lake Drive
Warner Robins, GA 31093
www.samhainpublishing.com

Print ISBN: 1-59998-430-X
Digital ISBN: 1-59998-188-2

Editing by Jessica Bimberg
Cover by Scott Carpenter

First Samhain Publishing, Ltd. electronic publication: February 2007
First Samhain Publishing, Ltd. print publication: November 2007

Chapter One

Katerina, Princess of Alluvia, took short strides alongside her brother and let one last voiced groan slip out. The painful headache she suffered left her rattled. Her hands trembled at her sides. She wanted to reach up and squeeze her head until the throbbing stopped. But her brother, Prince Balthazar, would not be pleased. He wanted everything to go smoothly during their evening ball. She'd heard the whispers among the nobles. Secrets were not easily maintained and, if they were, then suspicions were hardly ever far from the truth. Katerina had a notion her current stressful condition was brought on by the fact people knew she and her brother were looking over prospective suitors for marriage.

When the horns blared, announcing their entrance into the grand ballroom, she steeled her nerves against the earsplitting blast.

"Make them stop," she insisted through gritted teeth.

"Hang on, it'll end soon enough." Balthazar's hand discreetly encased hers as they stood in the arched opening.

She clenched her grip repeatedly in frustration and stared at the guests filling their palace. Her eyes burned with tears for the pain, yet not a drop spilled to her cheeks. If it killed her, she'd not let a single subject of her country see she had a flaw. They expected their princess to be more than perfect.

"There are so many," she whispered. "I hope they don't all get into the receiving line."

"I assure you, every eligible male in the place will stand forever, waiting to bow before you."

"How utterly sweet."

"You'll have to tone down your sarcasm, Kat, if you hope to find a husband."

"I wish they didn't know one of us has to marry," she whispered.

"They only suspect."

"That's as good as knowing for a fact. This is a full gathering of the highborns, no peasants, and their only reason for being here is by our invite. There is no holiday, no mention of a celebration of any kind."

"Alluvians like a good party." He nodded his head toward a few smiling ladies.

"They want to find out if the rumors are true."

"What if they do? Our goal to find a spouse is that much easier with everyone of quality in attendance.

The nobles of Alluvia stared with their usual intrigued interest. Their presence prevented her from taking any action that might lessen the throbbing tension blurring her vision. She saw them, each one with a distorted smile. How many stood with a false grin while plotting to take over her kingdom by marriage?

She didn't know Balthazar's thoughts on the matter, but she felt ill at ease about marrying and letting anyone into her life without knowing everything about them. That sort of understanding required a long period of time. However, the men she knew didn't interest her in the least. Many even repulsed her.

The trumpeters, in their fine plum attire, fitted with all the fancy ornaments, ceased making the infernal noise. The relief she received came in a small measured dose she had no appreciation for, except it led to another minute closer to the end of the evening.

"Shall we?" Balthazar directed her on the path through the crowd.

Katerina painted on her smile and nodded to the twin lines of well-wishers. Her hand slipped from Balthazar's casual hold, to the formal one of his forearm.

"Lord Granger." Balthazar paused. "It's good to see you up and about after that nasty carriage accident several weeks ago."

"Thank you, Your Highness. However, I regret I haven't the dancing feet for this evening."

Katerina glanced down at the man shaking a bandaged foot for their inspection.

Balthazar laughed lightly. "I do believe you will disappoint some ladies then."

"Never, Your Highness. I have other ways of entertainment at my disposal."

"Just be sure to rest your injured foot. Keep it propped up and give it time to mend. Come the full spring weather, and the snow has left us for good, you'll not want to miss out on the first hunt. The princess would miss you on opening day of the season."

"You've no concern there. I had every intention of keeping both my feet up." He grinned devilishly at Katerina with a nod. "At no time will I ever miss a hunt."

Katerina wanted to pinch Balthazar for playing matchmaker again. She saw it in the man's face and heard the secret scheme in her brother's voice.

"I don't like him." She hissed the words low when the man moved away. "He's too short."

"Posh. The man is as tall as you." He rolled his eyes. "You said not shorter."

"I said I prefer taller and I meant taller than me."

Katerina stared at the dais as if it was a sanctuary. Once she reached the top, she'd relax. Balthazar held her back, pausing at the base of the dais and she waited with him. Her brother, the diplomat in social affairs, always believed it best to acknowledge the guests with a bow before ascending to their lofty perch. He said it made them more human to the people they ruled. Except those in the room were nobility, the pompous mixture of lords and ladies. They weren't the peasants, the backbone of their existence.

She followed Balthazar's lead and gave a small nod to the left, then to the right. Her gaze locked onto one person. Dreamy couldn't be a word used for a man, it seemed—unmanly. Still, the word floated in place of conjuring another.

A crushing weight debilitated her normal breathing. His intense stare lingered with what she thought interest. Just when she thought her headache might wane in favor of this distraction, his gaze left hers. He whispered to the young woman next to him. Flustered by the mind-numbing throb to her temples, Katerina's outrage at his flagrant disregard left her empty inside.

"Kat?" Balthazar leaned close, nudging her out of a trance.

"Yes, I'm coming." She walked with him up the steps.

Her mind returned to their predicament. As much as she wanted to be ruler, Katerina had doubts as to whether she could perform when needed. Raised for the position, she and Balthazar were capable of accepting the esteemed honor as joint rulers. They worked well together and hardly ever disagreed about important decisions. However, it was decreed only one of them could ascend to the throne. Her heart wavered when it came to a single aspect of the duty. Was she capable of taking full reign of Alluvia? Would her migraines, with their searing pain, cloud her judgment?

"Our guests, sweet sister," Balthazar whispered without moving his lips. "Do they not look ever so happy to be here?"

His voice bubbled excitedly. In ways only she recognized, Balthazar was still her cute little brother. A year separated them in age, yet she always saw him as an adorable boy, never serious, never concerned over anything. She used to tease that their father found him in a snowdrift.

"Vultures," she replied. "Every man in this place is attracted to the throne and our coffers. None are interested in just me."

She resisted the urge to press her fingertips to her temples. The action would take away from her public appearance, not to mention ruin her neatly pinned coiffure.

"Ah, I think you must be wrong. The eyes of men don't deceive when they look at you, Kat." He nodded at the guard to allow the first guest to come up the short run of carpeted steps. "While I do believe you are right about them dipping greedy fingers into our finances, I believe they would first like to obtain a place in your bed." He snorted, a comical sound that irritated her.

"I wouldn't laugh if I were you. This wonderful lot of ladies does look below your standards. I'd like to point out those most anxious to have your favor are old enough to be our mother."

She didn't bother with a snicker when a woman approached them. The woman appeared quite ready to accept the prince in her bed if nothing more. The smile and giddiness were unsuited for the aging matron, but so typical of a lonely lady's attraction to a man. Balthazar had all the fine qualities of stateliness, including the handsome features people admired. If he wasn't so fun-loving and irresponsible, he might have had himself a bride before it had become a requirement.

She heard him swallow and take in the seriousness of the situation.

"Some warning about the succession could have been mentioned before Father's demise," he said sharply to Katerina under his breath while smiling at the oncoming woman.

Katerina's eyes watered. She loved her father and she doubted very much he expected to die suddenly. She liked to think he had every intention of letting them have as long as necessary to meet and marry in a normal fashion. She needed to believe that, rather than the idea he had purposefully left them both as contestants to the throne.

"Good evening, Countess Hortence." Balthazar bowed.

Katerina gave a tip of her head. Even that slight movement reinforced the sharpness of her pain.

"Good evening, Your Highnesses. I do hope I'm not too bold in offering my condolences on your father's passing. King Norvel was beloved by our kingdom."

"Thank you." Balthazar nodded.

"Such tragedies seem to abound for you over the years. First your mother's death..."

Katerina could have bust a gusset on her corset. The woman had no right mentioning their mother. Her passing many years ago remained a painful memory. Even to Balthazar, she suspected, when his hand clasped her fingers for comfort.

"Yes, but we all must part this world for a greater one." His hand clenched a few times and released. "Some are blessed to go ahead and make our road less troublesome when we join them."

"But for your poor family to lose a mother, a brother and a father is beyond the limits many of us could endure."

Katerina appraised the woman as an obnoxious nuisance with her morbid talk of death. While Countess Hortence's choice in topics appeared to be her tedious way of connecting with Balthazar's emotions, she couldn't have chosen a better way to alienate him. He never liked talking about death.

The woman continued to chatter, almost lapping at Balthazar's caribou boots in a bid to become his wife. The goal of becoming Queen of Alluvia was the dream of most women. Nevertheless, the woman had to be at least forty years older than Balthazar and the obscenity of even considering her left a sour taste in Katerina's mouth.

When Balthazar finally gave the woman a dismissive bow, she waddled down the dais with clear disappointment on her face.

"Father's rulership was commendable, but his edict for us is deplorable," Katerina fumed. "The idea one of us must marry to succeed to the throne is a troublesome annoyance."

"Don't look now, but I do believe it is your turn to be ogled closer than a prize ham." He lifted her hand and kissed her gloved knuckles.

"Oh, please, Balthazar. Could we not break protocol and dance?" She took a fleeting glance at Lord Henry of Elbian and Lord Thames of Alluvia advancing in the line of guests they were receiving.

"What of your headache?"

"I'd suffer worse having to deal with them." Her headache had come from the whole ordeal of searching for suitable prospects.

"As much as I'd like to break tradition, we are required to spend time greeting the guests."

"Not we, only one of us *is* required. I'll concede the position to you." She shuddered while trying to consider one of the two unsuitable men for her.

"Then dance away, dear sister, and have fun."

She looked at the line of men and women. The one man she'd locked gazes with before caught her attention. His disinterest hurt. As he fussed over his female companion's hair, Katerina decided he was a fop—a handsome man, but a bore with an ego.

"I'll stay." She twined her arm through her brother's. "My headache is too horrid to concentrate on dancing."

"Good. I could use the company." He rubbed her fingers. "Besides, in a short while we'll dismiss the well-wishers and you can discreetly slip out of here altogether and lie down."

He turned from her to greet the next in line.

Katerina's real excuse for remaining stood in that line. The popinjay had something intriguing in his stance and she had to meet him, regardless of the fact he came with a lady at his side. The reason was no doubt a form of self-torture, but she didn't care.

While he wasn't the only tall man in the crowd, he impressed her with his handsome features, much more than Lord Henry and Lord Thames ever could. They were older than dirt, uglier than toads and chauvinistic cretins. They also believed a country should only be run by a man. Their presence was one reason she didn't want to show any tears. The man she married would have more interest in her than ruling her country.

Chapter Two

Dax averted his gaze from the princess. Her youth and beauty made it seem strange she hadn't married. The information he had that she was a shrew might account for some loss of interest. However, men stared at her despite her temperament. Given normal circumstances, he imagined himself pursuing the Alluvian goddess.

"She's very pretty," Giselle commented, repeating his very thought.

"I agree and it's probably gone to her head—thinking she can get her way no matter what. I'd guess she's a spitfire in private and a man would do well to stay clear of her."

"Yet, you cannot." His sister coiled her arm around his and lowered her head.

Dax glanced up from Giselle's sudden shy retreat of observing the royals and saw the princess aiming a cold, hard stare at his sister. Giselle had a charming beauty all her own. Her pixie face and dark curls would make any woman jealous. He dared not think how ill-tempered Princess Katerina would be once he set his plan in motion.

"Remember your place and stay clear of her, Giselle. Katerina Romanoff is mine to deal with and she will not like our schemes."

"She's not the only one."

"I agree. It's bad form to deceive anyone, including the royals, but we haven't a choice if we're to follow this through 'til the end."

When the prince and princess mounted the stairs of the dais, Dax watched the princess openly. What he noticed first, what he found completely odd was her hold on her brother. Gripping tightly to his sleeve, she appeared ill. He studied her for the advantages that might give him in getting to know her.

When she turned, she apparently took a moment to compose herself. With her eyes shut and her jaw tensed, he wondered if the woman suffered mentally. It would explain the irritated, sour expression and the fact she hadn't married.

"You should have fun this evening." Dax diverted his sister's thoughts. "The prince appears to be a jolly sort and sports a dashing smile."

"He is the only thing I see about your awful plot I might enjoy. Except—" She hesitated.

"Except what?"

"Do you think he is intelligent enough to figure out your plan?"

"To be sure I'll need to meet him." Dax steered Giselle along the receiving line. "We will introduce ourselves. You'll bat those lovely eyes at him and gain his attention. Before this night is over, we will see who of us is the more cunning, the prince or I."

"She scares me."

"Princess Katerina? Why?"

"She just doesn't look the sort to let anything get by her."

"Oh?" He looked down at Giselle and her funny notion. "Why do you think that?"

"Because she has a far off gaze to her eyes like you get when you're dealing with important matters."

"And here I thought she might be sick." He took another inspecting glance at the princess.

"Oh, she is that as well. I do believe she has a severe headache."

Rigid, with a slight flush to her cheeks, the tint to the princess's pale skin appeared natural instead of applied with a hair-bristled wand. Her liquid brown irises shimmered and he guessed whatever her preoccupation lingered on, it didn't include the room full of people.

"I suppose you see a resemblance of how I look with a headache?" He noticed the lines of pain more clearly since his sister pointed out her suspicions.

"It looks extremely bad. I hope she doesn't cry," Giselle said with her usual sympathetic tone. "It would be such an embarrassment."

Dax nodded in agreement. He remembered the time he had a dreadful headache and cried in public. Of course, at thirteen everything embarrassed him when it involved humiliation.

When it came their time for introductions, Giselle walked up the steps alongside him. With her grace and beauty, he saw no reason for the prince not to take notice of his sister. From her perfect features to her infectious laugh, Giselle could capture a man's heart without trying.

"Your Highnesses." Dax bowed low as his sister curtseyed. "I am Duke of Maltar and I'd like to present my sister, the Lady Giselle."

"Maltar," Balthazar exclaimed. "What a distant land. I feel honored to have you join us and I see I've been remiss in visiting a place with beautiful attractions."

He took Giselle's hand and lifted her from her curtsey. His kiss smacked the air above her knuckles.

"Maltar boasts of many fine things," Dax replied.

"Tell me. Are the Northern Lights as brilliant from your kingdom as I hear tell?"

"Exquisite, but if you wish to see the full beauty of the Aurora Borealis, then might I suggest a visit to Volda. It has a perfect view from atop the Mezameer Mountains."

"Volda indeed is at the furthest reaches of the Aleutian Isles. I know very little of the place, but I'll keep the information tightly breasted for future trips I should make." The prince turned his head toward Giselle. "M'lady, have you been to Volda?"

Dax gripped Giselle's arm tighter as a small gasp started to escape. She didn't like to lie and he hadn't foreseen the prince interrogating them. His mention of Volda was evidently the wrong choice of topics.

"Volda is a lovely kingdom, Your Highness. It offers a great many luxuries not found on some islands," Giselle answered.

Dax noted how she had the prince captivated.

"What luxury is your favorite?" Balthazar inquired.

"The hot springs from the volcano."

"Ah yes, we have those here and they are quite wonderful." He bowed closer to her. "Very invigorating for a dip, but I hope you watch it doesn't scald your fine skin."

Dax let pass the mention of Giselle's nakedness. Her blush set the prince's interest aflame and it appeared they'd succeeded in overcoming one obstacle to his plot.

Dax turned his attention to the quiet princess. "How about you, Your Highness, do you also like the hot springs?"

"I like them well enough," she responded with a frigid tone of boredom.

Breaking her resistant aloofness could be a challenge and he decided the nudge she needed had to be drastic and out of the ordinary. With the prince being distracted by Giselle, Dax took the opportunity to step closer to the princess.

“I shoulder think with skin as milky white as yours, you might find the waters too blistering for your tender flesh.” He lowered his voice to an almost inaudible sound, allowing only her to hear him. “I hate to think of your breasts taking the abuse.”

Her velvet brown eyes widened, her nostrils flared and her chest heaved with indignation. He boldly watched her lovely breasts swell above the rim of her gown, presenting more of the creamy curvaceous treat for his eyes. When he directed his gaze back to her face, he saw his rudeness shocked her, but also seized her curiosity. He doubted any man talked to her as boldly.

“Your Grace,” the prince interrupted, “your sister has charmingly given me a complete itinerary of Volda. I’m fascinated by her knowledge of the place since Maltar is her home.”

Dax took Giselle’s arm. “Yes, well, she loves to travel and once she leaves the wonderland of your kingdom, she’ll tell everyone about its attractions, too.”

“We have a name for such a free woman,” the princess commented.

Dax narrowed his gaze on her. As much as he needed to charm the woman, he’d not let her get away with referring to his sister as a harlot. Royalty or not, her remark was impolite.

Chapter Three

Katerina took satisfaction in the way she dented the duke's overconfident attitude. It served him right to think the worst of her comment. His lewd compliment deserved retaliation.

"I beg your pardon, Your Highness?" His rich, baritone voice gave her goose bumps and his cool manner attracted her.

"We call them tour guides." She smirked.

His brow jumped and his serious glare receded into a humorous twinkle. For a moment, Katerina felt uncomfortable under his blue-eyed stare and the teasing appeal of his intense scrutiny. Her heart fluttered with excitement.

"Yes...of course." With his gentlemanly bristles eased, he turned his attention back to Balthazar.

He conversed naturally with her brother, as if they were equals by the standard of royals. Mindless of her surroundings, she listened. The romantic pitch of the duke's voice fit perfectly with her unfulfilled dreams. A shiver rushed her fevered blood.

She wished to turn away. Retreat from the duke who saw her interest in him. Each time her brother turned his attention to the lady, he missed witnessing the way the duke's roving gaze swept over Katerina.

In general, she'd found little in any man to give her stale heart a reason to pound with wild abandon. She could not ignore the duke's devastatingly handsome features. With wide shoulders, narrow hips and a muscular build, he was the man who could be her king.

The gleam in his gaze made her think he read her mind.

"Are you enjoying this evening?" Balthazar asked of Lady Giselle. "I would beg you to allow me the honor of the first dance."

"Thank you, Your Highness. You need not beg, I would like very much to dance with you."

"Your words make my evening ever more special." He lifted her hand and offered another proper kiss of air over her gloved fingers.

Katerina saw the spark of something special in her brother's brown eyes. His hand extended to the girl when she attempted another courteous dip to curtsey. He pulled at her to rise as if he feared she'd soil her knees. Katerina had never seen him smitten by any woman. Then again she had never seen one as lovely and unassuming as this delicate creature. She listened to her brother chatting with Lady Giselle. Had he talked this way with the courtiers or his occasional dalliances? Had she missed observing how he charmed women?

An almost mute twitter of laughter broke from the lady. Her voice tinkled like the tiny bells they used for dinner and Balthazar's face lit with the same glow Lady Giselle's radiated.

Katerina envied their thrust into happiness. She looked to the duke in anticipation of the same.

"Your Highness, it has been a pleasure." He bowed.

The slight rise to one side of his mouth mocked her restless heart. Then, he winked. She couldn't be sure since the brief flap of his dark lash went steady. Maybe he had a twitch or a nervous jitter. Or possibly, she had studied one eye too long and all he did was blink. He did have the most gorgeous cerulean blue eyes.

The duke broke from their staring contest and looked at his sister. Katerina accepted the victory and also turned her gaze toward the lady. It seemed the practical thing to do before the duke engaged her again with his hypnotizing, bejeweled gaze.

Nudging Balthazar, she nodded toward the receiving line of impatient people. She understood his reluctance. Lady Giselle's soft smile with her heart-shaped pink lips invited his full attention. The shy bob of her head and the slow bat of her lashes had him mesmerized. Another love-struck poppet fawning over her brother was one thing, but Katerina couldn't tolerate him playing the fool in love.

"Your Highness." Katerina spoke low, hoping for only him to hear her. "The line grows long with our anxious guests."

Discreetly, she watched the duke step back. His fingers circled Lady Giselle's elbow and gave a tug. He bent at the waist, low and submissive. Katerina found it rewarding, as if she gained some sort of respect from him. There was also the chance he mocked her with his contempt. Needless to say, it left a distinctive fervor in her belly—like butterflies and birds trapped together.

The duke slid a foot back, aimed for the first step. Lady Giselle gave another of her dips with her head bowed. When the duke turned to escort her down from the dais, his neck twisted, bringing his face around, and he smiled.

He left her confused about his feelings. His sister's interest in Balthazar, however, was unmistakably a mutual attraction. The petite creature had the beauty and poise her brother deserved. She was also meek and possibly introverted. A timid sister-in-law would be much preferred to a forceful one.

Gathering her wits, Katerina touched Balthazar's arm. "I'll stay if you'd like to dance with her now. She's pretty and you shouldn't let her get away. Another man might charm her into promises."

"No, I shall deal with this line. If your headache is taxing you and you'd like to leave, I can explain your absence."

"My headache?" She reached a hand up and smiled. "How odd, I find it is much better."

The duke successfully drew her thoughts from the stress of having to find a husband and it helped relieve the headache. However, she had another, deeper pain located in her lonely heart. She watched the duke take easy paces down the steps from the dais.

"Then you shall dance first," Balthazar insisted.

"Oh, but you should—"

"Do you really wish to stay and have a nice chat with your fondest admirers?"

"No."

She didn't need to look at the receiving line to know Lord Henry and Lord Thames neared the front.

"You'll go first, then," Balthazar repeated. "All you have to do is decide on an escort. Or—" He gave her a mischievous sidelong glance. "I shall."

Balthazar's laughter stabbed her with a quiet foreboding tremor. She hated when he was all too pleased with himself.

"Your Grace, one moment please," Balthazar called out as he picked up Katerina's hand.

"Oh no, I couldn't dance… Oh Balthazar, not with him."

"Do not think my mind so preoccupied with Lady Giselle that I didn't notice you find him attractive and he you."

Balthazar's voice lowered as he leaned toward her. "He's neither old, nor short."

"Really Balthazar, I dislike it when you foist me off on someone," she grumbled, nervous the duke might refuse to dance with her.

As a princess and one of the regents of Alluvia, protocol dictated he shouldn't decline. But it didn't mean her stomach understood etiquette.

"You'll thank me," Balthazar whispered in her ear.

Dax looked back. His sister made a small sound and he suspected she thought as he did—they'd been found out. It didn't seem possible that someone had told the prince they were not who they claimed to be, but he couldn't rule out the possibility.

Dax patted Giselle's hand and left her at the foot of the dais as he went immediately up the steps. The prince looked beyond him with a smile for Giselle and Dax's concern eased. The princess, on the other hand, appeared upset.

He took slow strides, teasing the princess with anticipation.

The fragrance of roses floated under his nose from the garlands above. He hadn't gotten close enough to the princess to know if she smelled as sweet.

The music in the room danced and circled his thoughts. Everything fell into his perfect plan. But, if she smiled, he'd see something of the scheme crumbling. He didn't have the sort of callous nature to trick a lady into losing her kingdom unless she had a personality as cold as ice.

"Your Highness, how may I be of service?" Dax stood prepared for any surprise.

He took a glance in the princess's direction. She had a way to make time stop. Her lovely eyes, full of woe and wonderfully perfect for her oval-shaped face, disturbed him. A cold-hearted woman would not have emotions parading across her face for a room of people to see. Did she sense his attraction and really experience tension and fear?

"The princess is in need of a break from her duties here," the prince replied. "I have insisted she move about freely and I thought you could escort her."

"I'd be honored." Dax tipped his head, but kept his eyes on the princess.

She appeared ready to bolt from the room in a fit of mortification. Maybe it would not be evident to everyone or maybe he read her wrong.

Dax offered his hand to her.

For a second, she stared at his open palm as if she didn't know what to do. Then she glanced at the front of the receiving line. He didn't know the two men waiting their turn. However, they looked perturbed by the delay. One incessantly tapped his boot, while the other kept scratching his short, pointed beard.

"Maybe you have a different choice for a dance partner?" Dax gave a jerk of his head toward the two men impatient for her attention.

"They can have a chance at her later." Balthazar shoved the princess forward. "I'm sure you will give her a much livelier step and not trample on her toes as they have before."

"You assume too much, Your Highness." She practically seethed like a boiling pot as she stumbled closer. "Maybe His Grace does not dance."

"I dance, Princess, but I dare say no one would suit you."

"And just what do you mean by that?" she demanded.

"Who but an angel could compare to your grace or give you the heaven on which you should waltz?"

On a slow intake of air, her lovely chest rose and fell with the splendor of her shapely bosom. Her arm lifted with a willowy elegance and her white-laced gloved fingers hung in front of him only for the second it took for his grip to give them balance.

The heat of his touch scorched Katerina's fingertips through the cloth of her glove. His gaze held hers and neither spoke. His care at placing her hand on his forearm sent shivers to her toes. Her feet didn't move upon first try and she looked to her brother. His smile of triumph, the gloating gleam in his eyes, all reminded her he knew her well. She felt absolutely silly with the effervescent giddiness churning her insides.

"Princess?" The duke's voice broke through her thoughts.

"Yes." She bowed her head and let him lead.

Holding lightly to his sleeve, she glanced at the old men, the strange men and the ugly men in the winding row along the wall. The Duke of Maltar fit in no category but that of his own.

"Shall we dance?" he asked. "Or would you prefer to do something else? I'm at your complete disposal."

"A dance will suffice."

She moved her hand up his arm and curled her fingers along the firm curve of his bicep. The muscle twitched beneath the tight fabric and she felt a quiver in the sensitive area of her intimate regions. When he said complete disposal, her immediate thoughts jumped to his lips brushing hers. She hadn't been kissed in a long time.

Katerina looked at the guests enjoying themselves dancing. When the duke led her to the middle of the floor, he politely waited for her to approve his embrace. With her nod, she slid into the circle of his open arms and they enveloped her in a warm and secure hold.

"You were wrong to think I need someone better to dance with." She gazed up into his face, appreciating his height.

"Was I?" His mouth lifted at the corners, deepening dimples in his cheeks. "Maybe it's not been long enough for me to take a misstep or squash your delicate toes."

No sooner did he mention clumsiness, than Katerina made a blunder, placing her foot on his shoe. She shivered with the thought everyone noticed and furthered her embarrassment by stumbling into him. The duke drew her against him and she forgot the crowd. His eyes were the only ones that mattered.

"See how clumsy I've been. I apologize." His fingers glided the length of her spine.

"You needn't be so gracious about my...my..." Words failed her.

His head lowered, placing his exquisite mouth within inches of hers. Full, sensuous lips beckoned hers to taste them.

"Your Highness, might I suggest we either dance or move off the floor before we're trampled?"

She nodded, though it meant losing his tender embrace and relinquishing the idea he would kiss her. Shaking the silly wish from her head, Katerina took his arm and walked with him to the outskirts of the throng.

The chatter of ladies around her offered both good and bad tidbits of opinions. On one hand, she triumphed and had the envy of all the ladies of the court. The duke was the epitome of handsome masculinity and she was the one attached to his arm. On the other hand, everyone thought she was colder than an Aleutian winter night and she didn't deserve him. It hurt, even though they might be right.

"Your subjects find you very beautiful," the duke commented.

"Thank you, but it is not *my* face they are impressed with."

"Then it must be mine," he chuckled, and nodded to ladies they passed.

She had fallen into his charming trap. The duke had the attention of many ladies and Katerina didn't feel comfortable with him noticing.

"I referred to my station, not your swaggering vanity, Your Grace."

"Please, call me Dax." He laughed.

Servants had it easy where social gathering was concerned. For a whole second she thought how nice it would be to toss aside the decorum of nobles and royalty. Yet, calling him Dax would be an improper breach of etiquette. It opened her emotions to a vulnerability she didn't know how to handle.

Chapter Four

Dax hadn't expected the princess to be beautiful. He knew nothing of Katerina when he came to Alluvia and beyond her appearance, she had an inner quality he found appealing—loneliness. He identified it well from experience. She wanted someone to cherish her for herself and not for her position or wealth. That awareness made him feel off balance dealing with her, because he wanted the very same for himself.

"Was your journey here uneventful, Your Grace?" the princess asked, not responding to his bid for a more personal acquaintance.

"Won't you even try to call me Dax?" He slipped his arm around her back and drew her against him as if they were going to dance on the sidelines of the ballroom.

"I'm sorry, Your Grace, but it would not be proper for me to address you so informally, nor is it appropriate for you to hold me this close."

He waltzed her along slower than everyone else danced, steering her farther from the view of her brother.

"Proper and appropriate are what you make of it, Princess. You appear capable of deciding for yourself what is suitable." He gave in to decorum and danced her into the crowd on the ballroom floor. "Unless you're...never mind."

The princess's soft brown eyes looked up at him with greater interest than he expected. All his information about Princess Katerina of Alluvia had, of course, been tainted by the source. She could hardly be considered a shrew or cold-hearted. Not when she gazed at him with the lustful passion of a woman willing to compromise her reputation. She spoke of them being too close, but not once did she try to remove herself from his embrace.

"Or what?" Her sweet breath fanned his face.

"Or, Your Highness, might I suggest you are uncomfortable in a man's arms?" he teased.

"I've danced in the arms of many men and I see no threat to be in yours."

"And your heart?" He pressed his hand to her back, forcing her to feel the pounding of his heart upon her breasts and discovering hers rapidly beating, too.

"What does my heart have to do with dancing?" Her eyes grew curious with a delightful sparkle, as if she were an innocent child.

"Does it always beat this fast and hard, as if trapped in a cage?"

The princess shook her head violently in several short turns. Two curls sprung free and bobbed over her left eye. Her silent protest spoke the opposite of what she wanted him to think and know about her.

Dax put a hand up and tucked the curls back into the arranged swirls. He didn't tell her how soft and silky the strands were—his attraction grew strong, like she possessed the magic to put him under a spell. He enjoyed the sensation of happiness, but now was not the right time to forget he worked toward destroying her to save his kingdom.

Wherever they went, the sea of people parted like two waves. Dax and Katerina moved carelessly between the wakes. The brightly lit room concealed nothing about the woman. She carried herself as regally as any noble. Her willowy figure intrigued him enough that he overstepped boundaries, sliding his hands wherever he pleased.

On the small of her back, he felt the heat of her body. Endowed with a healthy set of breasts on her sleek, streamlined frame, the way the princess had them cinched up in her clothing appeared to be uncomfortable. Taking note of the soft ivory swells made his cock stiff and his erection battle the cloth of his trousers.

"Might I suggest some refreshments?" Dax didn't wait for her answer. He needed a drink and a reprieve from her delicious, warm body rubbing his.

From a servant passing by, he plucked two long-stemmed crystal flutes from a tray. Handing one to the princess, he took a swig from the other. Over the rim of the glass, he watched Katerina's mouth part. The fine crystal touched her dusky bottom lip and she tipped the glass, gingerly sipping the wine. Her tongue peeked out and ran a slow trail over her top lip. The elegant drama enchanting him didn't end when she took another sip and the bubbles tickled her nose. She lifted a hand immediately to ward off a sneeze she didn't get to stop.

Dax put a hand to hers, holding the glass to prevent her from spilling the drink. He looked deep into her wonderful stare. A hundred places to kiss her and he thought of nowhere else than the tip of her nose. At the first chance he got, he would.

The princess shivered.

"Are you cold?" He continued holding her hand on the glass stem.

"Actually, I'm quite hot."

Her warm, wine-flavored breath caught his and tugged encouragingly at his lips. With little effort on his part, he could have her against him. From toes to nose, he wanted to meld their flesh with the thrill of passion.

"That doesn't seem hard to imagine with all the people in this room generating body heat." He envisioned his tongue thrusting between her slightly parted, plum-tinted lips, tasting the wine the way she had.

Dax discarded his fluted crystal on the credenza next to him. Then, right as her eyes blinked, he put a hand on her hip and one between her shoulder blades. The princess slid her foot closer. Her thigh brushed his and her breasts pressed against his chest. The pearlescent skin rose above the edge of her violet gown. He recognized her perfume as an infusion of rose petal water—a scent he never appreciated until now. Something else had been added. After another deep inhale, he suspected it was the natural fragrance of her sex.

Katerina's hips shifted and he moved his leg, accommodating her fit and sensing a preclimactic tension. He forced his knee against her gown, into the juncture of her thighs. She took a deeper breath. Her glassy gaze held a blend of trepidation and confusion. His stance blocked her from public view. Though not enough to prevent a passerby from seeing their closeness—tightening, aligning and fitting together as only lovers should.

The tragedy of Katerina letting the duke kiss her would be, she'd love it. She'd adore the moment, the man and the sensations of being a woman. Then he'd abandon her. She didn't know much about men, even with her brother's antics giving her insight as to what they were like. He showed sweet devotion to one and then another without ever realizing the consequences to the woman.

Katerina looked into the devil's blue eyes. Each time his fingers moved, she repositioned. Every time his body twisted, she turned to fit. The pores in her skin dampened and she shivered again. Expectation and desire held her back from the boldness of begging him to kiss her.

"We're too close."

"I know." He had his hands in all the wrong places for public appearance.

"You should move away."

"Or you could."

She looked at his naturally tanned skin and the hint of whiskers peppering his jaw. His eyebrows were combed flat and his teeth resembled polished chips of white marble. Only someone so near might notice the hair in his nose was clipped. Yet, she didn't want anyone else to be as she was, where his lips might touch hers or their lashes fold together. Fantasies rose high in her mind. For once she didn't force them away.

The duke's hand squeezed her bottom and she heard an embarrassing moan escape her throat. As if testing her voice, he kneaded the quivering cheek of her ass again, pulling and forcing her tighter into his crotch.

His other hand slipped up her back. Scorching fingers folded around the nape of her neck and held her head firmly. She couldn't begin to think where she should put her hands.

"If I don't move, what will you do?" Her body went through a series of titillating sensations in response to the heat between them.

She had forgotten the glass in her fingers until the duke wrenched himself away. He claimed the glass from her fingers, tipped it to his mouth and swallowed the remaining drops of her wine.

"You were asking of our trip here," he reminded her.

Katerina turned away. Unable to think, tense from a shuddering orgasm, she gripped the edge of the table for balance.

"Oh?" She held back her tears, using the hate of rejection to dry them. "Yes, yes of course I was."

She froze the moment he stepped behind her. His hands stroked her arms and she involuntarily leaned on him. The twitches of her insides weren't nearly as much a problem as the slow trickle of wetness leaking from her undergarments or the way she writhed against his solid body. Her knuckles blanched and her nails bent near the breaking point.

For a long moment, they stood silent. Katerina indulged in her ongoing fantasy that they were the only two people in the palace—on Earth. And then she heard the music, the laughter of people making merry.

"Please," she whispered, hoping he'd leave her to deal with her embarrassment alone.

He released her, but he didn't leave. She needed to say something to keep the silence between them from unnerving her.

"If you have something to share about your travels here, I'd be very interested. I so seldom get away from the castle, let alone take a trip upon the Aleutian Sea. Even then my journey has never been farther than the outlying islands and close neighboring kingdoms. Maltar is an extremely long distance off and I've never come...I mean I've never gone close to that island."

Chapter Five

When Dax, nearing his own erupting climax, set the glass aside, he didn't realize how upset the princess would be. She rambled to fill the silence and he couldn't callously let her believe the moment hadn't affected him.

"We have some magnificent sightings of whales. Giselle loves the big creatures and if possible she'd have one as a pet." He laughed nervously.

The sweet nectar of Katerina's femininity clung to his nostrils. He put a hand on her shoulder and slid it down to the bend of her elbow. Her flustered moment compelled him to offer support.

"They are quite splendid to behold."

Her gaze scanned the area nearest them.

He had already conducted his own survey and found no one had any particular interest in what they were doing. Maybe a gentleman or two watched and suspected. Yet, no one would dare speak of such a thing without more facts.

"I must excuse myself." The princess's face flushed pink.

"I'll take you." Dax held lightly to her elbow and led her from the ballroom to a ladies toiletry room.

"I can manage to find my own way back to the ballroom," she announced in a dismissing tone. "After all, this is my palace."

Her dilated eyes danced, gazing everywhere, except at him. He gave a nod and she disappeared behind a door. Dax never had the shame of awkwardness before. The innocence of her expression touched him. Her discomfiture tightened his lungs, making it difficult for him to take a deep breath.

Dax could not leave her unescorted.

He walked a path back and forth over the fine Persian rugs. Lighting a cigar, he puffed on it profusely—a nervous habit. Twice he considered following the trail of the princess. After twenty minutes, she emerged with another woman.

"You're still here." She looked surprised.

"Yes."

"Henriette, would you excuse us please." She touched the woman's hand on her arm.

Dax waited until they were alone before moving toward her.

"I wouldn't have taken so long if I'd known you were waiting." Her gaze dropped to her hands and back up with an apparent worry. "You were...waiting for me, weren't you?"

She looked frightened for that one second. Her throat jiggled up and down with her swallows. Her eyes watered. He couldn't know or understand what she felt at that precise moment, but if it was anything close to the way he anxiously awaited her acceptance or rejection, then he sympathized.

"Yes." He stubbed out the cigar in a crystal dish. "Shall we return to the ballroom?"

Winging out his elbow, he gave a smile that drew her to him with a magnetic swiftness. His stomach churned with indefinable emotions. All would be lost if he gave into the feelings he didn't want involved. Someone should have warned him his heart could never be hardened against falling in love.

The duke possessed a lethal calmness that attracted Katerina. She let many events overwhelm her, while he made everything he experienced appear like it was nothing. His composure exuded elegance and his attentiveness toward her, though rough around the edges, charmed her.

She compared him to a boy she knew from years gone by.

Stefan was seventeen and she sixteen when he caught her eavesdropping on the king's indiscretion with a servant long after her mother died. Her punishment had started out as a kiss for his silence and that almost led to her losing her virginity. In those minutes of innocent experimentation, Stefan changed her. He forced her down on a settee and managed to push the summer gauze of her dress past her knees, above her thighs. Her head swam in clouds of confused infatuation. Before she knew what he meant about kissing her other lips, her legs were spread wide and hung over his arms. His kiss pressed to the mouth of her sex's inner lips.

To struggle or not was decided by a swift and intense orgasm. Her limbs went weak, yet her hips vaulted to claim his thrusting tongue. Stefan's sweet suckling had been the start to a good many years of self-induced rapture. His image blurred with time, but the lasting results were in place for her to pleasure herself until she writhed on her bed in the middle of the night. The duke's face would now make the ideal replacement to those late night fantasies. Imagining his mouth in place of Stefan's added the maturity she needed to stimulate desires of intimacy.

Once they entered the ballroom, the duke's embrace for another dance came without question. He watched her too closely for an excruciatingly long time. What did he scrutinize so thoroughly? Her mind went over the details of her face. A nose too narrow, cheekbones too high, and her mouth drooped in the corners. Balthazar said it was because she forgot to smile.

"You're staring and I find it rude." She felt under too much pressure.

He had broken down all her self-assured control and she needed to gain it back. Her best defense was to be offended by everything he did or didn't do. She didn't know how that would help her, but it worked thus far in keeping her resistant to his odd sense of humor.

"As I said, you're quite nice to look at and I do not ever deprive myself of something as lovely as sunshine."

"Thank you." She tipped her head slightly as the compliment softened her mood.

Her pulse increased, outrageously thumping the palm of her hand on his shoulder. With errant disregard, her heart quickened. Her body went on another sinful trip to respond to the duke in every way possible.

"It was merely a comment so don't flatter yourself believing I'm trying to please you."

Katerina's frustration escalated. One minute nice, the next arrogant, the duke seemed intent on confusing her.

"It must be a great pleasure to find that I am not ugly, since you have traveled far to compete to be my suitor," she retorted, not understanding why he would try to insult her.

He stopped dancing and held her steady. "Conceit is an ugly quality, especially in a princess."

"I'm not—" She lowered her voice. "I'm not conceited."

His laughter flowed with an offensive loudness. Abhorrently thunderous, his voice equally matched the pitch. "I am in no way interested in courting you, Your Highness."

Katerina's ears pricked to the instant murmurs around her. The gossips clucked amongst themselves about the duke's harsh honesty. Katerina wanted to scream at him a thousand obscenities, yet the penetrating spell he held her under with his delicious eyes kept her silent. Her attraction remained steadfast as she imagined the deep rich blue would be fitting beneath a king's crown.

The magic swept her beyond madness and left her little sanity to think and she grasped for his reasons to make the comment.

"You're married then?" For pride's sake, she said it loud enough for the rumormongers. She needed to offer them a reason for the Duke of Maltar's public rebuff.

Katerina took a deep breath waiting for his answer. A yes, would put her out of her misery.

"No." He made it sound common knowledge.

"Engaged?" She grasped for another route to re-establish her dignity.

"Not even a hint of such." He stopped and bowed when the music paused. "Shall I take you back to the prince or do you wish to fend for yourself. There appears to be a great flock of admirers from which you could pluck your own escort."

"You ill-bred oaf." The words seethed low through her clenched teeth. "It would be rude of you to leave me in the middle of the ballroom. I insist you take me back to my brother."

He offered his arm and her jaw clenched. His form of humor annoyed and upset her. Reluctantly, she put her hand on his arm. If not for the need for decorum, she'd have him flogged for his flagrant announcement to everyone within earshot that he did not consider her worthy of him.

Imagine, her, the Princess Katerina, Regent of Alluvia, not good enough for a duke. How dare he suggest it, she silently fumed.

Chapter Six

No longer pale, the princess had all the coloring of an enraged inferno. Dax lifted a hand to her cheek to catch the tears her eyes tried to squeeze back. The impulsiveness of his move startled her and she flinched.

"Don't," she ordered.

He never found himself in a position to take orders. Ignoring her demand, he wiped the wetness from her smooth skin.

"I can't have you crying or your guards might think I'm the cause."

"I have a headache and you have no effect on me."

He stared at her distressed eyes. A headache or not, he was the cause, and out of compassion he needed to be the cure.

"Allow me, Your Highness." He massaged the pulsing skin near her hairline.

He didn't take his gaze from her face even though she looked around.

"People are watching." She expressed some annoyance.

"Yes, they are and always shall."

Her brow furrowed in confusion.

"You're a very beautiful woman and worth more than a glance."

He smiled, noting she didn't retreat from his finger pressing her temple in a swirling fashion. It didn't matter to him that they stood in the middle of the ballroom gathering attention. The princess was his concern for the evening.

"So?" He made the same motion over her other temple. "Do you care what these people think or would you rather accommodate your comfort."

Thinking the princess favored being pampered, he didn't expect her to slap his hand away. Not only did she communicate her apparent indignation with a small noise and a wrinkled face, she trotted off for the dais. Bumping into the unwary, Princess Katerina wove through the crowd like a bad seamstress wielding a needle. She zigzagged all over the place as clusters of people deep in conversation didn't notice her approach or move out of her way fast enough.

Not one to insult the royals totally, Dax followed her. He nodded an apology for his own crashing course through the regrouping of people.

"Your Highness." He grabbed her arm firmly before she made the bounding leap up the steps to the platform where her brother stood.

"Let me go."

"You're overreacting."

"You know nothing about me. You chose to insult me and you know it." She wiggled her arm.

"I used a poor choice of words."

He eased his hold when he saw her consider his apology. Without further word, she spun away and trudged too quickly up the steps of the dais on her own.

The inevitable conclusion to Katerina's night would be complete mortification. The hem of the dress caught beneath her shoe and it seemed fitting to top all other embarrassing moments with a grand finale. The spectacle could be her retiring exit as she bounced down the steps bottom side up. Except as she fell back, hands grabbed her from behind and her teetering steadied on the gold carpeted tread. She wanted to bestow a thousand kisses on her rescuer.

"Watch your step, Princess," the duke whispered near the back of her neck.

His breath blew a feathery dusting of air over her skin. The fine hairs on her nape fluttered. A shiver teased her spine as he held her hips longer than necessary or appropriate. She turned to face him and her belly twisted into a ball of knots. His hands lingered in touching her.

Memories were wickedly inconvenient when it came to his long fingers stretched over her bottom. He stood one step below her and it still put him tall enough to be eye level. His effort to preserve her stateliness could not be overlooked. Yet, what could she offer? He didn't want her, nor did it appear he wanted to kiss her. He'd had the opportunity and broke from it as if he saw a wart on her nose. His hands dropped away and she instantly missed the heated contact.

"Thank you." A dizzy euphoria swept through her.

His smile wasn't condescending or brusque. Instead, the warm, considerate expression warned her of the danger he presented. She clutched the front of her dress, unsure what else to say to him. If her headache hadn't returned, if he didn't behave so strangely, she would be calmer.

"I am your servant, Your Highness."

The duke lifted one of her hands and his action brought an end to her abusive wrinkling of the fine silk. She watched him.

Hypnotized by his bow over her trembling fingers, she wished his hands were back on her hips, her waist and...oh how she wished, she didn't have on gloves.

Her breath caught the moment his mouth pressed audaciously tight to the back of her hand. He kissed the lace covering her knuckles and lightning skittered up her arm and stabbed brutally at her soul which longed for love.

"You have my gratitude, Duke." Prince Balthazar pulled Katerina up the last two steps to him. "May we offer you a reward for your quick action?"

"That will not be necessary, Your Highness. I'll always find it the greatest of pleasure to be of service to the princess—any service she might request."

Katerina made no mistake this time in seeing his one eye crinkle closed for a half second. The duke had definitely winked. The sparks of attraction ricocheted wildly inside her. His cool blue eyes twinkled like exquisite gems. The slight curve of his mouth held a sinful grin. She couldn't think for a minute what other services he could be of use for, if not marriage. Then her brother's cough brightened the burnt-out light in her head. The duke's impertinence left her speechless. Her brother's amusement upset her.

To add fuel to the fire the duke added, "Besides I'd hate to see her bounce down the stairs head over heels. It would forever overshadow your magnificent ball."

Katerina growled low. Balthazar bobbed his head in agreement with the duke and she fumed in silence. The lock of hair fell from her coiffure and she pushed the obstinate curl back into place. The duke successfully ruined her fantasies of him. Each time he spoke, her heart lurched at the appealing resonance of his voice but he trampled the allure by some twisted sarcastic wit he thought he possessed. He treated her as if she were the one behaving like a spoiled child, when he insulted her every chance he got.

"Dine with us," the prince commanded. "Tomorrow, eight o'clock and please, I insist you bring your lovely sister."

"It would be our honor."

Katerina's shoulders dropped. Her mouth would have too, if she wasn't already clenching her jaw in aggravation. She looked at Balthazar and saw his attention focused on Lady Giselle who danced with another gentleman. Indeed, the mutual attraction was highly evident. Balthazar appeared too eager when the girl's gaze lifted shyly. The coy move of lowering her lashes again seemed planned.

Was Katerina the only one seeing the feminine wiles of the little seductress? Or was she overreacting because, while she recognized how ladies flirted, she wasn't good at using such devices?

Katerina didn't want to believe her brother had overlooked the duke's lewd insult. Yet, she saw Balthazar's mind preoccupied by the graceful fairy-like lady waltzing around the room. The dinner invitation was his way of getting closer to Lady Giselle.

The duke backed down the half dozen steps. His gaze, an inferno of promises for her, alluded to the decadent sins she had very little knowledge of and even less experience. Tomorrow seemed a lifetime away.

Chapter Seven

Dax purposely took the slow, measured steps needed to continue teasing the princess. He'd brought her to a private ecstasy and left her simmering like a fine stew.

All banter up until then had been politely blunt. She didn't hide her anger well and he really hated to see such a statuesque maiden crumple at his offhanded comments. If there were any other way to gain her undivided attention he would have taken it. But he knew how much he detested people who spoke to him as if he needed to be coddled during every conversation. For Katerina it would be no different. Everyone would be kind and polite and do her bidding because she was a princess. What she needed was someone to stimulate her mind, giving her a reason to take more than a mild interest.

Any other time, under different circumstances, he imagined himself on bended knee, begging for her favors. Only he had been warned she had the personality of a termagant. She could be selfish, willful and unpredictable. Thus far, he'd seen little of those poor qualities.

Dax watched Katerina, with her stiff posture and commanding carriage, move across the dais in her regal attire with poise and grace befitting her station. The pretty violet gown complimented her curves. The color left a reflection upon her skin—a radiant glow like the Aurora Borealis on the snows of

Volda. He had astonished her by not kissing the moist lips she offered. More so, he had surprised himself, because for an instant—no, for a whole minute—he debated kissing the sweet breath of the princess until she beseeched him to carry her to bed.

"Dax, Dax, would you look at the lovely rose the prince gave me." Giselle flew at him as if she had wings on her heels.

"Very nice."

"Why, you haven't even looked."

Dax turned his head and glanced at the ordinary flower.

"Smell it." She held it to his nose. "Isn't the fragrance absolutely wonderful?"

"Very nice, but if you hadn't noticed the whole room has hundreds."

"Yes, I know, except this one the petals are almost heart-shaped. When I pointed it out to the prince, he climbed on a chair to pick it from the arrangement himself." She sighed.

"How chivalrous of the prince." He took her arm and moved away, out of the princess's sight.

"I saw you with the princess." She smiled. "Were you not afraid she'd think you too bold by holding her hand that long?"

"Never mind how I deal with the princess. Are you playing your part well?"

"Oh, Dax, Prince Balthazar is so nice." Giselle clutched his arm. "He said he looks forward to seeing me again."

"Yes, and he's arranged that by inviting us to dinner tomorrow."

She sniffed the flower again. "He's sweet and kind and..."

Dax took her chin and held it up. "Don't look too desperate to please him, Giselle," he instructed. "He's used to being pampered and indulged by pretty women. You need to keep a reserved politeness."

"Nothing is ever right enough or perfect enough for you. She smacked his arm.

"I'm sorry, Giselle."

"You should be. At least the prince likes me. I didn't see you win over the princess. She practically ran from you."

"She's a bit high-strung and very emotional."

"Maybe you should be more charming and stop putting her on the defensive."

"You could be right. Yet, this is important and she's better off staying a bit confused by me. I've given her enough reason to be attracted by being different than anyone she knows."

"I think she'd be attracted to you even if you were yourself. Every woman in our own kingdom thinks you're handsome, including me."

"You're biased." He plucked the fingers of Giselle's gloves one at a time until the lacy covering came off.

"See, another reason for her to like you. You're not conceited."

"I don't believe Katerina would quite agree with you on that point." He kissed the inside of her hand and considered what the princess's hand might look like without a glove. Would she have the smooth velvet skin of his young sister? Katerina wasn't old, but some would consider her beyond marrying age. Her advantages were her position and her beauty.

"If you ask me, you should stick with the old saying, you catch more flies with honey, than you do with vinegar."

"How would she know how sweet I am if she didn't have a taste of bitterness?"

"We are doing the right thing, aren't we?"

He knew they weren't, but now wasn't the time to upset Giselle.

"We're doing what we need to do and before you know it, we'll be sailing home with this all behind us." He tickled her palm with another kiss. "You'll have the prince eating out of the palm of your pretty little hand tomorrow night. As for Princess Katerina, she's already primed for the next phase. Have no worries, she likes it better that I'm not a humdrum suitor."

"Could you imagine if he really did eat something out of my hand, the future King of Alluvia." Giselle giggled with delight.

"He'll not be king, Giselle. Remember that is why we're here. We have to prevent him and his sister from ever being crowned."

"I know, it's just a thought."

Before he responded, he saw Lord Talbot stride toward him.

"Excuse us, Giselle." Dax pushed her to go.

She glanced over her shoulder and then back to him. "I don't like that man."

"I'm in a hundred percent agreement with you there, now go on." He watched her until Lord Talbot blocked his line of vision.

"She's such a pretty little thing, but is she clever?" Lord Talbot's fingers brushed over his fat moustache.

"My sister has no reason to be clever." Dax folded his arms over his chest.

"Prince Balthazar is no fool, or at least his sister makes sure he's not looked upon as such. Can your sister keep him from finding out our plans?"

Talbot's gaze went to the dais where the prince and princess sat talking.

"Giselle will do as I tell her and the regents of Alluvia will never know the extent of anything until it's too late. We've made our deal and unless you want to make them suspicious, you should avoid being seen with me." Dax dropped his arms. "As you've noted, the princess is observant."

"Just remember our agreement, Daxton. I want this country. It should have been mine and if I had known of our family's secret law about being married to rule, my younger brother would have never gotten control of these lands."

"You have Elbian. That island far surpasses the size of Alluvia, so why the need to have more? You've rejected the title of Prince of Alluvia."

"Alluvia has wealth, while my island was founded by criminals exiled there."

"Regardless of Elbian's colonization, you're the ruler and could be called king."

"I'll never be called king until I'm crowned King of Alluvia."

"You still haven't explained why I'm involved." Dax glanced at the princess on her platform, greeting guests.

"Because you come from a small, nothing of a place, which I can easily overtake with my army and you'd rather have a peaceful resolution to your problem than fight me."

"There are closer islands, small kingdoms. I don't think I still understand. Why me?"

"I know Katerina and her quirky dislike of men shorter than her."

"And my stature is a reason?"

"Among other things. It happens a cousin of my wife visited Volda and couldn't stop gushing about how handsome you were. In great detail she gave me all your attributes and she is much like Katerina, hard to please."

Lord Talbot walked off with a satisfied smile and Dax couldn't help think Talbot was deceiving him just as much as the regents. When he looked for Giselle, he saw her dancing. She'd not lack for a partner. His eyes went to the princess and it settled his decision. He had to take better hold of the reins of his future.

The crowds of people in their finery moved for him as he hurried to make alternate plans from those he had previously made with Lord Talbot.

Dax found the cloakroom and his coat. "The coachmen." He dropped the heavy fur coat into place as his arms slipped in the sleeves. "Where are they?"

"If you'll give me your name I could—"

"Where?" Dax snapped at the servant.

"I'll show you m'lord."

Dax followed the short man. Unbeknownst to Lord Talbot, Dax began to formulate his own agenda. No more would he be the puppet Lord Talbot controlled. The princess's country was in just as much trouble as Dax's and he needed to help her.

He went with the servant and found his hired coach, along with two men from his ship.

"Junroe, you and the lad return to the ship and prepare to set sail in two nights." Dax ordered the captain.

"Where to?" Greever asked.

"We go home and if things go in my favor, we'll have guests."

"Who?" Greever's youth got the better of him.

"None of your business, boy." Junroe gave the lad a warning glare.

"Aye, Captain."

"You don't want us to wait and escort your carriage back to the place you're staying?" Junroe asked Dax.

"No, Giselle and I will manage on our own. I want there to be no delay in leaving when I get on the ship. We don't know if this unusual shift in the weather will hinder your travel to the wharf."

"We'll get there quicker than a wink."

Dax patted the man on the shoulder and returned to the ballroom in search of Giselle. He debated when or what to tell her. She'd not like his change in plans.

Chapter Eight

Katerina continued her discreet search of the ballroom. She didn't want the duke to catch her looking for him. She studied every group of people, each shadowed corner and repeated the inspection.

Earlier she saw the duke talking to his sister. Once they faded into the crowd, she hadn't seen either of them.

"You didn't have to invite him to dinner," she admonished her brother during a lull in their talking to others.

"Didn't I?"

"Give him a medal, part of the kingdom, something, but please, rescind your invitation. He humiliated me out there and I've no wish to dine with him." Her foot tapped silently in vexation when she recalled how loudly the duke had announced he didn't want to court her.

"I didn't ask him solely for you. I wish to get to know his sister."

"You could have invited just her."

"With no escort?" He lifted her hand and kissed her knuckles. "Besides, dear sister, I think you protest too much. The duke looks at you as if you're already his."

"Ha! He said he wouldn't court me."

"Maybe his wish is not to be trapped into it. Courting is such a ritualistic word. I don't like the word myself. It makes me feel as if I must follow an archaic standard of etiquette to win a woman's hand."

"If I haven't been too blinded by my headache, I see the Lady Giselle as the winner. You could have thought of another way to court her without my involvement."

"Honestly, Kat, do you think I know you so little that I'd not notice the man has your full attention?"

"He doesn't." She groaned with the lie. "How could I ignore him? He's left me little choice but to watch for his rudeness."

"Face it, the man has gotten under your skin and you like it."

"I'll admit no such thing." She folded her arms with the adamant statement.

Balthazar's soft smile, his understanding and his knowledge of when to back down from even the smallest of arguments made her give a little.

"All right, I find him a teeny bit handsome."

"I'd say he's got a whole lot more than a pretty face to make you this anxious."

"He's not—"

Balthazar held up his hand. "Enough. I've an urgent matter and it's your turn to guard the throne."

"Urgent matter, my foot... Oh go on with you, before she gets bored waiting for you to trip over yourself vying for her affection."

"I only wish to have the pleasure of a dance."

"Now who's glossing over their feelings? Besides, all you need do is command her and she'll have no choice."

"What tact you have, dear sister. I suggest turning on the charm if you want the Duke of Maltar to take more notice of you."

She watched Balthazar look around to spot his quarry.

"She's too young for you. I highly believe she's a virgin, an innocent girl of maybe sixteen."

The idea of endless encounters with His Grace brought her headache back immediately.

Balthazar took Katerina's arm and wrapped it around his. "What is this? Jealousy? You cannot stand to have my interest taken from you. Therefore I must forgo delighting the beautiful Giselle?"

He raked a hand through his thick, short-cropped brown hair. His overconfidence mirrored the duke's. They were handsome, roguish men no one would change. It made her wonder if she'd been too hard in her judgment of the duke. Perhaps her nervousness made him as anxious.

Katerina looked for the duke in the horde of twirling dancers. The splash of colorfully dressed people made locating him difficult.

"Do you see him?" Balthazar gave her a teasing nudge.

"I wasn't looking for anyone in particular."

"Can I not pry a little confession out of you?"

She looked at him and smiled. "No."

"Fine, remain stubborn, but I know he's the first man you've taken this much interest in for a long time."

"What will I do for fun when you marry?" She thought changing the subject would be for the best. "I'll be bored senseless."

"You could marry the brother." Balthazar guided her to her chair. "I do believe he can be every bit as entertaining as I am."

"I may have considered it until the lout opened his mouth when I asked about him being a suitor. He said he had no desire in marrying me."

"I highly doubt that, after the way he teased you."

"He said it loud enough that everyone heard, Balthazar."

"I didn't."

"That's because the Lady Giselle has you captivated by some mind-numbing enchantment and you listen for only her voice."

"We were discussing the duke's eligibility and suitability as a husband."

"There's nothing to discuss. I've never been so mortified. If it was his intention to tease me, he could have picked from a hundred other things."

"You're too sensitive. He doesn't know one of us has to get married."

"Yes he does and so do all the other people here. Gossip travels fast." She plopped down on the cobalt blue velvet cushion and kicked at the little stool for her feet.

"I think you'd be surprised by what he thinks of you. Steal a glance, take several. You fascinate him and I see that every time I catch him looking at you." Balthazar lifted the lock of hair dangling over her eye. "A man might not always admit when a woman strikes his fancy. Fear of commitment has a way of paralyzing our common sense."

"What's he afraid of? I don't bite and I'm easy to get along with."

Balthazar laughed with the same outrageous humor the duke possessed. He knew her too well. But she was in a foul mood.

His smile softened. “Maybe he’s playing hard to get. You know, men do like to be chased by pretty girls.” He kissed her gloved fingers. “Now excuse me while I take a turn at pursuing a very lovely young lady.”

“I won’t chase after him.” Katerina bolted up out of the chair, her voice a little too loud because he walked away ignoring her.

A guard stepped forward. She laughed, looking back at him. Tall, neatly attired in his uniform and too immersed in his duty to watch for any real threats. He had only heard her rise in tone, not her comment. It amused her in one way and irritated her in another. His boredom made him lax in his position.

“Step back,” Katerina commanded with a wave of her hand. “You look ready to slay my admirers.”

She painted on her best smile and looked at the receiving line. Lord Henry lingered in the same place, letting others go by him while she’d been gone. He waited for her and she had no choice than to give a nod, allowing his approach.

She sat back down on the tufted seat.

“My dear Princess Katerina, you are more spectacular looking than the last time I saw you. Each passing day you age with grace.” He bowed and kissed her gloved knuckles.

She raised a brow. The oddly insulting compliment made her sound ancient.

He slobbered profusely, wetting the thin cloth, and she grimaced at the dampness seeping through to her skin. Did men realize they merely kissed over the last kiss left there to dry?

“Thank you, Lord Henry. You’re the same kind and handsome man as always.” She stared at him and thought about him as a husband.

He would fit the position as the queen's consort. Only she was young and had many years ahead of her. Did she want to have a husband who appeared to be a shriveled up walleye and was probably just as slimy to kiss?

Her consideration of kissing led her to scour the room for the duke and he was nowhere to be seen. She watched a cluster of four young women. Their giggles and gaiety made her wait and observe who entertained them to the point that they were not interested in her brother.

Not to her surprise, the duke emerged with one young woman who he spun out onto the ballroom floor. His head came up as if his sixth sense detected Katerina's hawk-like surveillance. He tormented her with a smile, gave a nod acknowledging her inspection and resumed his conversation with the woman in his arms.

Katerina ached to feel the strength of his graceful guidance waltzing her anywhere he chose. She shivered remembering the smell of him. The heady fragrance of his cologne blended nicely with the natural oils of his skin. She even liked the hint of the cigar when she'd returned from freshening up.

Beneath the candlelight of the chandeliers, the duke's silky black hair shimmered. She dreamt of twirling her fingers in the locks framing his angular face, knowing it would be as soft as it appeared. She had many fantasies about him building in her mind.

"...so if you would like to dance." Lord Henry continued to talk without noting her indifference to his presence.

"No. My time here has been too brief as of yet. But I do thank you." She gave him her hand and he deposited another wet kiss on her glove before leaving her.

Katerina blindly waved on the next in line while trying to watch the duke move around the room. However, the pompous

Lord Thames planted himself in direct line of her gaze. After him, a half dozen others interfered with her view.

Chapter Nine

Time had a way of moving too slowly and at the same time speeding along. Dax saw the night escaping. He had to capture Princess Katerina's complete attention.

From the sidelines of the ballroom, Dax watched Giselle's smile glowing brighter than the chandeliers overhead. She had no experience with men—no sense of right or wrong when she let her feelings guide her. She waltzed around the room in the arms of the very attentive prince. It concerned him at some level. His chaste sister, still a child to him, had a woman's age, and he worried she'd get hurt in all the trickery.

The music paused and the prince led Giselle toward him.

"Duke, I return your sister unscathed by my two left feet.

Dax gave the man a nod of his head and took Giselle's arm.

"This is such a lovely ball, Your Highness," Giselle's voice bubbled merrily.

"Thank you. Should I have known such beauty would be here, I would have ordered up every rose from the royal greenhouses to be placed in this room." The prince smiled.

"Then there might not have been any room for me," Giselle replied.

"Oh no, my lady, there would be no room for anyone but you...and of course myself." He bowed. "Alas, the room is full and I do have a duty to perform. If you'll excuse me, I should return to the princess and dismiss the remaining guests from the receiving line. She needs time to enjoy herself."

"I understand she has headache," Dax pried.

"Yes, dreadful thing she gets. The royal physician says it's stress. She never used to get them this bad before our father passed. Now...well Katerina is very brave. To present herself to the public while enduring the pain is admirable. She makes me proud to be her brother." The prince leaned toward him. "Don't let her ruffle any feathers, Duke. She's only testing you for endurance. Beneath her stony exterior, Kat has a tender heart."

Dax found the information useful. Yet, looking at the dais and the tranquil expression on the princess's face, he wondered if she was all her brother thought. The woman he watched showed signs of weakness where her feminine side hid. However, it didn't mean she had a tender nature.

◆

When Balthazar bounded up the steps two at a time, Katerina saw the little boy in him again. His face aglow, his smile wide, it made her heart light with affection.

"I think she may be the most perfect creature in all the world." The statement rushed out on his excited breath. "She's young, but eighteen in a couple months is not too young and she pleases me."

"I'm happy for you, Balthazar, if she's the one to marry."

"What do you mean if? It's not like we have much time to be choosey."

"We also don't know anything about her."

"She's from the Isle of Maltar."

"So we've been told."

"And what's that suppose to mean?"

"We've never heard of her or her brother before tonight. I should think you might question the duke's ancestry, his title, the family background." She took his hand and looked at the ring on his middle finger with the royal seal of Alluvia. "What if Lady Giselle and the duke are charlatans?"

"I see no reason to disbelieve who they are."

"It was just a thought, Balthazar." She rubbed her finger over the stone in the ring. "I suppose not knowing any Maltarians makes me a little suspicious to have two become quick acquaintances." She touched her own ring, a daintier duplicate of Balthazar's that she'd inherited from her mother. Twisting the gold band, jeweled with diamonds and a large amethyst, she felt a little sad knowing she'd have to give it up. If Balthazar did marry first, it would rightly belong to his queen.

"We have a month left before one of us must marry to take sole rule of Alluvia." Balthazar sat in his chair next to hers.

"Why do you suppose father did this to us? As his son, you should reign over Alluvia."

When the king died, Katerina thought it the worst day of her life. Her father naming Balthazar and herself as joint rulers for one year caused a big dilemma. In that year's time, whoever should marry first would be crowned king or queen.

"It's the law," he answered.

"A law no one knows about except the rulers. He could have easily chosen you to secure the future of our kingdom."

"Not without me being married."

"Easy enough, he could have ordered you to marry."

"Father loved us equally. He was a forward thinking man and believed it would be favoritism for him to select."

"And thus he burdens us with this choice." She picked at the fringe on the chair.

"Kat, he was trying to be practical."

"Then he could have come up with something other than a contest."

"This is not a contest because we are not in competition."

"Not with each other, but we are against time."

"We've only ourselves to blame. The time was there, we grew lax in deciding how to go about doing this." He patted her hand. "Everything will be all right."

"But, I don't want to get married, not yet."

"You won't have to if I marry first. Though, I've always thought you were better suited to ruling the kingdom than I am. I prefer—"

"Having fun."

Balthazar shrugged and gave her one of his adorable smiles. "You know I was quite content with us jointly governing our kingdom."

"Yes, and we do it well together."

"However, the deed is done and father's bequest is final. He wished for one of us to marry to meet the guidelines of the law."

"And if neither of us should marry within the month, Uncle Talbot, who is next in line for the crown will take over our kingdom."

"The law is clear. The ascension of a prince or princess to supreme ruler must have a spouse to help ensure the continuation of the bloodline."

Katerina looked across the room at Lord Talbot. He stood grim-faced, yet eager to see them lose the kingdom. His wife, their aunt, was a conniving, short round sow of a woman who always stirred up trouble. Even at a distance, Katerina imagined the woman talking rubbish about Balthazar and herself.

"He no longer calls himself prince. Therefore, I do not see where it gives him any privileges here. Look at him, all smug as if he knows he'll get what rightfully belongs to one of us."

"Forget about him and come dance. You've sat here long enough. There are plenty of potential suitors for you, even if they are not up to your standards."

"I've heard they find me scary."

"Then let us show them you're as sweet as honey."

Balthazar waltzed her around the ballroom and she relaxed, finding peace in the security of her brother's strong arms. Whatever doubts she had in him becoming ruler were mild concerns, such as letting some of their overbearing lords talk him into rulings not beneficial to the kingdom. Fortunately, she'd be around to advise him. He always trusted her judgment.

In looking for the duke, Katerina took a moment to examine Lady Giselle. The young woman possessed many qualities Balthazar deserved in a wife. She would be a good choice since he already displayed more than a passing interest in her.

"What are you thinking?" Balthazar asked while they danced.

"That there's someone else you'd rather spend time with."

"Am I that transparent?"

"Uh-huh." She kissed his cheek.

Katerina and Balthazar had always been much more than brother and sister. They were friends. Even after they married, she knew the affection between them would not spoil.

"Why don't you dance with her again?"

"Because my first duty is to you." He looked beyond her. "Until someone takes you from me, I'll be your companion for the evening."

"You make me feel like an unwanted old maid."

She took a daring glance at the duke and found he lounged against one of the large stone columns supporting the ceiling of the room. His posture was relaxed and he appeared to have no cares. He didn't even have a gaggle of ladies surrounding him. It appeared as if he was bored with the whole evening.

"That's what you'll become if you don't give some man a chance to get to know you under that heartless persona you wear like a shroud," he warned.

"A real man would step up to the challenge. Unfortunately, we have sops in our hierarchy. Not one of them is bold enough to cut in on us for fear of offending you."

"That could be true, yet you're the princess. You could give one simple nod of your head to any one of them and they'd come to your waiting arms."

"Very well, I shall." She looked around for a rescuer, but she had pretty much deterred every man there by refusing to let go of her brother. Each tip of her head and polite smile only got her the same in return.

"You've alienated them all, Katerina." Balthazar laughed when no one put a foot in her direction.

"There's one man who delights in tormenting me." She took Balthazar's arm and led him to stand before Giselle. Then boldly, she turned to the brute capable of putting the sizzle in her temper as well as her soul.

"Your Highness." The duke righted from his slouched position on the pillar and bowed with a nod of his head to her.

Katerina waited for Balthazar and the Lady Giselle to leave before making her request to dance with the duke. Balthazar's enthusiasm sparked a little courage in her.

Chapter Ten

Dax didn't say anything as Katerina marched up to him and his sister. Once the prince left with Giselle he waited for Katerina to speak first. She appeared ready to bust at the seams to ask him something and he refused to make it easy for her. He had hooked her by alternating between kindness and arrogance, knowing the intrigue might excite her. Giving her his silence now added to her apparent frustration, since she didn't rush forth with her question.

"Your Grace." She fidgeted with her gown and the plum ribbon beneath her fingers came undone.

"Princess."

Something fearful in her stare kept him open for surprises. She expressed her interest well, each time her velvet brown eyes glistened with exasperation.

Her chin tilted up and her inhalation took a long time to fill out her bodice.

"Would you dance with me?" The words spilled from her lovely mouth in a wave crashing to his heart.

"Always an honor, Your Highness." He offered his hand instead of his arm.

The intimate gesture of handholding tested her without words. The personal, brazen and dangerous request would be regarded as insulting, or irresistible? He recognized the adventurer in her the moment she asked him to dance.

His hand was large in comparison to the slender one that slipped into his palm. Her lace-wrapped fingers curled around his.

"Don't you have anything to say about me asking you to dance? You've had a nasty comment about everything else I do." She turned into his embrace and they began to dance.

"Have I been cruel to you, Princess?" He laughed lightly. "And here I thought I was being honest."

The music slowed in tempo and he drew her closer. His heart quickened to match the beat of hers upon his chest. He actually held her too close to be proper, yet she made no protest. Her breath, flavored with a sweet brandy, appealed to his senses. Tasting her lips, sampling the flavor, became a distracting invitation.

"I did not appreciate any honesty you think I may have needed."

"I beg your pardon then, if I've offended you with my jests."

The lilting music, the flickering candlelight and Princess Katerina's beautiful eyes inspired him to behave...for a little while. If the intensity with which she looked at him hadn't muddled his brain, he would have come up with a dozen reasons he had to stay far away from her.

"Could we go out for a little fresh air?" The red tint to her cheeks suggested she was embarrassed by her possible misjudgment of him.

Dax led her to the balcony doors. "It's cold out there. Maybe you should get a wrap?"

He held the door wide. The frigid air swept through the room and he witnessed dozens of people shiver at the sudden temperature change.

"I'll be fine. I like the cold." She brushed past him onto the stone balcony.

Katerina hugged the thin, violet gown to her body. He snorted with amusement, but refrained from commenting.

"It's snowing again." He made the inconsequential remark while searching for a less heated route for any conversation they would have.

"Yes." Her wistful sigh softly shaped her mouth into a smile.

"It's a reminder it's still very cold." He scooped up a fistful of snow and formed a snowball. "I prefer summer."

"I like the way the whiteness covers up all that is ugly." She ran her gloved finger through the snow that dusted the stone railing.

Dax threw another snowball into the garden. It landed haphazardly in an urn and he noticed her smile widen.

"I really did aim for that."

"Sure you did." She laughed.

He had a plan and it involved control over her emotions. Her laughter threw an obstacle in his way. For one second—for one excruciatingly long moment—he wanted to make her so happy she'd never stop the enchanting sound of her genuine amusement. It also made her deliciously attractive beyond her physical beauty.

"Seasons speak of personalities, Princess." He shook off his inward delight and refocused on his task of keeping her confused by his intentions. "Are you frigid with a heart of ice?"

Dax took out a cigar and lit it to avoid looking at her changed expression.

"I'm...I'm not frigid." Her breath stuttered.

"Good." He held the cigar between his teeth while leaning on the baluster.

"I don't need your approval." She stayed silent for a long time before asking. "Why do you say it's good?"

"Because I wish to know you better." He puffed on the cigar and blew rings over her head. "Your gala looks to be going well."

He nodded toward the ballroom filled with happy dancing feet and enough chatter to last a lifetime. He didn't want a conversation and yet he drew her into one. He had to know if he could pull everything off without her suspecting she'd become a pawn in a game. What better way than to toy with her?

"I think everyone is enjoying themselves." She rubbed her arms.

"Yes, a right nice market of flesh for you and your brother to pick a spouse from." He blew another ring of smoke out, letting it swirl in front of her.

"Pardon me? That is not what this event is for."

Katerina wheezed when the smoky mist dissipated.

"No? My mistake then."

"It is merely a ball to formalize the transition of power from our deceased king to the prince and myself."

"That power, as you say, is already known by everyone here. What of the peasants? Maybe you should have had a grand bash to include the people you rule and those you wish to stay loyal to you." He spit a bit of tobacco from his mouth into a potted bush. The conifer dusted in a pretty white powder of snow, now had an ugly brown stain on it.

"I'm cold." She wrapped her arms around her shoulders tighter. "If you were any gentlemen at all, you would have offered me your jacket."

"What, so I could freeze?"

Regardless of his comment, he took his jacket off and laid the fine woolen garment over her shoulders. He smoothed his hands down the sides, not once but several times, to warm, to comfort, to prepare her to be teased much more than she could handle.

"Better?" He looked down at her while his hands rested on her shoulders.

"Yes...thank you." Her breath came in short pants of steamy air upon his face. Her fingers gripped the edge of the jacket and touched his.

"I'm at your service, Your Highness."

When she turned to face him, he stepped closer to the rail and poked his cigar into the snow. He neared her again, put the stub in his jacket pocket that hung over her breast and smiled. The dart hit home and he saw how she favored his closeness and how he couldn't resist her beguiling beauty.

"Excuse me, but I hate to waste and I assume I'll be getting my jacket back."

"A noble trait, something my more wasteful subjects should consider."

"Do you find the people not using everything they are provided with?" He slid his fingers along her shoulder until one brushed her neck.

"Nobles, not commoners," she replied. "Do you know I saw one of my lords toss out a basket of greens rather than give it to his servant?"

"Maybe the food was bad."

"I inquired and he said the abundance could not be just given away. He offered it for sale to the man and when the servant had no money to purchase the luxury, the lord simply disposed of the food."

"You could have ordered him to give it to the servant."

"I do not interfere in the households of my lords. Would you wish for me to step over your threshold and tell you what to do in such a circumstance?"

Dax brushed the pulse in her neck and studied her mesmerizing velvet brown stare. She hungered as he did for the kiss they needed to share. He tried to sort out the pros and cons of the undertaking. Would she hate him as if he were some rogue salivating over her like a fresh venison steak? The desperation for affection in her eyes, irresistible and demanding, tightened a noose around his neck. The cravat had a stranglehold and he slid a finger over the knot to jerk it a little bit free.

He could hardly breathe, she stood that close. The rose water she wore, faint in the icy night, enticed him to lean forward, inhale and savor everything. Her lips parted, begging for his. It was not what she should want or what he should do. Only she apparently didn't care.

Dax reached for a lock of sable hair, loose at her temple. The obstinate curl had plagued her all night. He had watched her on several occasions tuck it back in place.

Sliding his finger down the side of her face, he watched her cool skin flush a deeper red. The princess stood rigid. In fright or fancy he couldn't tell until his stroke took a route down her slender neck and she swallowed. The action produced a quiet hum. Her eyes closed and he turned his hand over to pet the smoothness of her breast swelling over the brim of her gown.

He leaned close. His nose acquired a fresh perspective of her scent. There, at the intersection of her shoulder and neck he began the trail. Her head tipped sideways, giving him access, opening the way for his breath to warm her pulse. That heat and steam produced a whimper and he waited for her to move first.

"You smell nice," he whispered.

A sputter of excitement caught her breath and her chest rose. It took a long time to fall away from his caress. He dipped a finger below the brim of the bodice and hunted for the prize. When his middle finger swept deep and hit the peak of her breast, Katerina squeaked and tried to draw back from the titillation hardening her nipple.

"I need no further investigation to know how your firm, ripe body needs a man." He laid his tongue over her racing pulse and licked the length up behind her ear. "Now let me hear you beg me to satisfy your hunger."

"I—I can't." She tried backing up.

The stone wall of the palace stopped her.

Dax lifted his head to see if she really wanted him to stop. Her eyes were squeezed tight. Droplets of tears in the corners prepared to freeze. He honestly didn't know if he could live with himself, causing her anguish. The indecision hung heavy until she looked at him. He wiped with a gentle flick of his finger at the leakage. He closed the space between their faces and brushed his nose alongside hers. Soft and tenderly he nuzzled the opposite side. She whimpered one short sound.

Her sweetness panted breathlessly ready for him to have her. He dragged his lips over her cheek. Not in a kiss, but a caress. Her fingers inched up the back of his arm drawing him to her little web of innocent lust.

The danger of affection grew. Dax stood straight, unyielding to his desires.

"I should take you back inside. You'll never get a husband standing out here with me."

The princess obviously yearned to be kissed but he couldn't do it. Not yet, lest it spoil his plans. Her face displayed immediate embarrassment from his rejection and he prepared for a thunderbolt to strike him dead for hurting her.

Chapter Eleven

The duke took Katerina's arm and jerked her from the wall. He offered no apology for his seductive taunting. With her mouth hanging open in shock, surprise and mortification, she wrenched free of his hold and pushed through the doors back into the ballroom.

Abruptly, she stopped, shrugged the jacket from her shoulders and held it out to him. "I wouldn't want you to go around telling people I stole your clothing."

Tears of frustration burned her eyes. Not wanting to run, she still took quick steps and made sure she didn't stumble going up the dais. Dropping into one of the two matching blue velvet throne chairs, she sniffed the air. The lingering scent of the duke's cigar had journeyed with her and she looked up at him.

"Your Highness." He bowed from the waist with a deep, almost groveling lowness as he stood on the top step.

She hadn't expected him to follow. When she waved her hand at him to not speak, she realized too late, he thought it a dismissing gesture and it sent him away.

Katerina wrapped her fingers around the arms of the chair and pushed herself up.

"Your Grace." Balthazar's voice stopped the duke at the base of the dais.

Katerina saw her brother come forward from the dance floor with Giselle. She held her breath in hopes her brother might find a way to prevent the duke from leaving. As troublesome as the man made himself, she had a great desire to be near him.

"Your Highness." The duke gave a nod of his head and took his sister's arm.

"Lady Giselle, until tomorrow." Balthazar kissed the girl's hand, bowed and strolled up the steps to the throne.

Katerina tried to smile when the duke's gaze met hers. She wanted to give him ever opportunity to change his mind and remain at her side. But, her mouth wouldn't work and numbly, she watched him lead his sister away.

For the rest of the evening she looked for him in just the same way as Balthazar studied the people for a sighting of Giselle. The hour grew late and Katerina felt disappointed.

"I believe they have left, Balthazar."

"I think so too," he replied sadly. "But that is good. I wouldn't want the Lady Giselle to tire herself."

She smiled, imagining the duke making the same sort of comment about her. A laugh followed at the absurdity. The duke had his moments of exquisite charm, but she doubted he'd worry over whether she tired herself for any reason.

The receiving of guests was over and done. Katerina sat quietly watching the nobility and their gaiety. The duke had given her a lot to think about. Aside from his brusque manner she had caught snippets of what happiness felt like. Those moments were few, but they were about to be spoiled by her uncle making his brazen approach.

"Let him say one word about Father and I'll have him ejected from the palace." The bitter words flowed through her gritted teeth.

"It would only make him happy to have you lose your temper, Kat." Balthazar waved Lord Talbot up the dais.

If it were left to her, she would have told the guard to show her uncle the door. Like a vulture, he came to pick at them. The last time she had any sort of conversation with him was at the reading of her father's will and the decree for one of them to marry. He'd said unforgivable things about her father and she'd not stand to hear more.

Lord Talbot ascended the dais at a leisurely pace. He moved as if he owned them and everything in the kingdom. He took all night to approach them, waiting until they were exhausted in body and weary of mind. However, her uncle didn't know how his presence mentally stimulated her thought process.

"Good evening, Your Highnesses." Lord Talbot's smirk was pure evil.

Katerina thought in a million years of knowing the man, she'd never see the attraction his wife did. With a long pointy nose and a wide lipless mouth beneath a bushy, gray moustache, he looked nothing like her father.

It made her think of the duke and what she found the most pleasurable—he had no facial hair. He had no ticklish moustache or sideburns looking like twin legs of a wooly lamb, and no chin whiskers to catch every crumb of food missing his mouth. On his head though, was a devil's mane of rich black. Feathery wisps layered all the way to his wide, thick shoulders. Her fingers twitched with the thought of sifting through those silky locks and pressing her nose into the softness.

"I'm sorry it's taken me this long to pay my respects. Your ball has gone very well I think," Lord Talbot said.

"Extremely well." Katerina offered her fingers as a way to flaunt her power with the ring of Alluvia.

Lord Talbot took her hand and bowed only, with no move to kiss her knuckles or the ring on her finger. The attempt to undermine her cool collected front had been wasted. The duke and his contrariness had toughened her spirit for this moment.

"I see the date you step down from the crown is nearing quickly." His bluntness didn't shock her.

"Or to a marriage," Katerina added.

"Yes of course. Do either of you have an idea which way that will go? I've heard virtually no rumors tonight about either of you. Well, save the Duke of Maltar confessing to have no interest in wedding you. Imagine my surprise when an eligible man would snub the princess."

"I was not snubbed. His Grace was every bit a gentleman, he just didn't suit my—" She tried to find the right words. "He is unavailable, that is all."

"Unavailable? That's an interesting way to describe a man who is neither married, nor betrothed, nor has any attachments." His amused laugh was discreetly low.

"I have prospects if you must know, Uncle. I have—" God how she hated to say their names, "I have Lord Thames and Lord Henry vying for my affections. Both are advantageous prospects if I should select one of them to be my husband."

"But you shall not, I think."

How did he know her so well? She was not close to him. Other members of his family maybe, but never Lord Talbot.

"I don't believe you know the extent of what I might sacrifice for my kingdom."

"Clever point, Katerina." He bowed to them both and backed down the stairs.

"You said nothing in my defense," she hissed under her breath to Balthazar.

"And get him started in on me. No thank you. You were his target and you handled him as wonderfully as you manage everything."

She lifted her hand and pressed her fingertips to her temples as the pounding began to escalate. The headache had waned in the presence of the duke only to return when she separated from him. The concept he could be a cure-all had earmarks of a ludicrous fantasy.

One last time she looked for him.

☙ ❧

Dax helped Giselle with her clothing since she had no lady's maid to assist as they prepared for dining with the prince and princess. He went over every moment he'd spent with Katerina the night before and knew this night would be harder. She'd be ready for his rude conduct and he didn't exactly have a plan for how to control that part of the evening. For all he knew, after a night's sleep, she woke with a decision not to join them for a meal.

But no, he pushed that idea away. After all, it was his rescue of her from falling down the steps of the dais that got him the invite. She'd be showing poor hospitality not to attend the dinner.

"Dax, I don't think I can do this. Prince Balthazar is very nice." Giselle held her arms up while he tugged her corset closed.

"It's only a few weeks."

"What happens if the prince and princess find out?" She turned around and put her hands on his shoulders. "Will they put us in prison? Can they execute us?"

"I'll not let any of that happen. One of them must marry before the end of the month and presently that's all they have on their minds. You entertain the prince with your charm and I'll keep the princess amused."

"She didn't look very happy with you."

"Princess Katerina needs a complex form of stimulation."

"You make kindness sound complicated. Maybe she requires love."

"We're not to think of such emotions with them, Giselle. We have one purpose with respect to our association with the regents. We ensure that neither marries so Lord Talbot will not attack our home."

Dax lifted Giselle's dress from the bed.

Lord Talbot and his army were large and powerful against his kingdom's small resources and it pained him to imagine what his homeland would look like if attacked.

"She's pretty."

"Who?" Dax pulled the gown over her head.

"Princess Katerina, silly."

"She's too pretty. That kind of attractiveness is always surrounded by a haughty form of conceit. Every beautiful woman I've known believes their looks should get them anything they ask for."

What he said of the princess fell far from the mark. She was not unfeeling and cunning. He had gotten close enough to see her vulnerable side and the loving heart she hid because she thought she must to be ruler.

"I saw you take her outside on the balcony," Giselle continued. "She was wearing your jacket when you came in. You like her." She held Dax's hand and stepped up on a chair, letting him straighten out the hem of her gown.

"She was cold and insisted on taking it."

"You're lying. You can't go fibbing to me, Dax, and get away with it. That little dimple in your cheek appears." She laughed, poking his face.

"Let me see how you look." He twirled his finger for her to pirouette. "Splendid. You're more beautiful than Princess Katerina."

Giselle giggled and jumped off the chair into his arms.

"Giselle, you're going to ruin the gown. We did not come here with your whole wardrobe." He hugged her tightly. "You just be yourself and you'll have the good Prince Balthazar drooling over you like a boy after a puppy." He let her slide down the front of him to stand on her feet.

"Dax, what if I don't remember everything you taught me. How to sit, which fork to use, and what if I should spill something? We never lived with such refinement." She frowned. "Though I wish we had."

"Hey there, my pretty pixie. You're a princess in all your actions as much as Princess Katerina." He held her chin and looked into the dark brown eyes. "Keep a watch on what Katerina does. She'll have impeccable table manners, just don't follow too closely or she'll think you mimic to mock her. Remember, they are people and have to chew just like us. You'll have time to eat, enjoy and digest everything they expect of you."

"I don't like it. He's so nice." She spun around. "It was like dancing on a cloud when he waltzed me around the room."

"After the end of the month, he'll be deposed along with his sister, and he'll not have time to think of you."

"Yes he will. Once he finds out what I've done. He'll hate me."

He had no argument. The prince and princess would never forgive the lies.

Chapter Twelve

The dinning hall lighting was low. A few candles and the fireplace gave the room a personal touch. Katerina worried over whether the duke would think it looked too seductive and, at the same time, she hoped the soft ambiance put her in a better light.

The night before, the duke's presence lent magic to the evening. Unfortunately, it also paralleled what might be considered a wicked dream. She had trouble understanding his motive for intentionally upsetting her. From the second he pretended to like her, to the minute he seemed to hate her, she felt pulled between horses by his indecision.

"The Duke of Maltar and his sister, the Lady Giselle," were announced at the door of the great hall.

Balthazar fidgeted with the sleeves of his jacket.

Katerina brushed his arm with a soothing stroke. She had never seen him nervous to receive a dinner guest. Then, it had indeed been rare for the guest to be a pretty marriage prospect. She had known one day he would wed, she just didn't know how to react to the idea he might fall madly in love with the woman he chose.

The duke bowed and Lady Giselle curtseyed. Protocol dictated that Balthazar take Katerina into dinner, allowing the guests to follow. Instead, with his head in the clouds and his heart on his sleeve, Balthazar took Giselle's arm.

"May I escort you?"

Giselle's fingers couldn't have moved faster to grip his arm.

"Leaves just us. If you'd like to latch on, we'll follow." The duke flapped his elbow upward.

Katerina lifted her arm to place it on his and then put it down to her side. "I can manage to walk on my own, thank you."

She strode away from him. The click of her heels made an annoying sound she never liked. However, she was not going to let him insult her each private moment they spent together. If Balthazar could break protocol and leave her to her own devices, then she would do the same and fend for herself.

The long banquet table had always meant to hold exactly thirty people. Balthazar, looking for the intimacy of a closer gathering, had the servants set up a small seating arrangement in front of the large fireplace. He held out a chair for Giselle and then seeing how Daxton lagged behind Katerina, held a chair for her as well.

"Is something wrong?" Balthazar whispered in her ear.

She shook her head and patted his hand on her shoulder. There would be no greater satisfaction than to have her brother personally toss His Grace out on his ear into the snow, whereby he could freeze to death. Nevertheless, the smile Balthazar had for Giselle kept Katerina silent. She'd not ruin his evening.

"Duke, please tell us of your home." Balthazar motioned for the servant to pour wine.

"What is there to say? It's not any different than here." The duke lifted his glass, swirled the amber liquid and took the customary sniff before sipping.

“There must be something unique about the place,” she commented. “I’ve never been there, however I hear the shoreline is smooth and sandy unlike our rocky cliffs.”

“I was not aware you had cliffs.”

“Oh yes, some splendid rock formations and panoramic views,” Balthazar exclaimed. “I should like to show you. Tomorrow! Yes, tomorrow morning. You shall stay the night and then we’ll ride by horse...or perhaps the ladies wish to go with us and then we could go by carriage.”

“I’d love to go.” Giselle smiled. “By horse would be fun...oh, unless Princess Katerina would rather go by carriage.”

Katerina didn’t want to go at all. The thought of being trapped in the carriage with her brother and his soon to be paramour, as well as the insufferable duke, made her queasy.

“By horse would be pleasant,” she agreed reluctantly.

“Oh, but we can’t stay here, we haven’t any clothes with us.” Giselle’s features expressed a genuine dismay as she looked to her brother for a remedy.

Katerina wanted to laugh the moment Balthazar’s voice broke the silence with a ready solution. He had to have been prepared all along with his answer.

“Not a problem. There are always armoires filled beyond capacity with clothing for just such instances. I’ll have servants show you to your room later and let you peruse the garments. Take what you’ll need and what pleases you, for they are yours when you leave.” Balthazar’s fingers slid over Giselle’s.

Katerina looked up from the oyster soup to see if the duke noticed the affection between her brother and his sister. It clearly could not be mistaken. The attraction grew with great speed.

Staring at the duke as he slurped the liquid from a spoon, she took in his handsome features. The dimples in his cheeks when he smiled warmed her insides. It wasn't until she looked away from his full lips to his eyes that she realized he watched her.

Katerina pretended indifference to his enigmatic grin.

Throughout dinner, the duke, in what she deemed his ever endless quest to annoy her, not only ate his soup noisily, but constantly dropped his napkin or utensils on the floor.

Katerina's groan of utter aggravation never drew Balthazar's gaze from Giselle. If he ate, it would be through osmosis, because Balthazar never lifted a utensil.

When the duke's napkin fell to the floor a fourth time, Katerina had enough of his antics. She put her hand on his to prevent him from retrieving the soiled linen.

"Please, let us get you a clean napkin," she offered.

"No need to bother."

"But I insist."

"Really, I've hardly touched that one to my lips."

His gaze dropped to her hand. She looked down at her gloved fingers on top of his. The thin cloth allowed her to feel the heat and stir of his knuckles as he moved his fingers.

"Please, a fresh napkin would be best." She lifted her hand from his and waved for the servant to do her bidding.

"I assure you, this one will be fine." The duke leaned from his chair.

Katerina placed a bite of her buttered bread in her mouth and nearly choked when he put his hand on her knee. Her sharp breath forced the food into her throat and she made a small cough to reclaim it before inhaling it into her lungs. The duke took his time fetching the cloth from the marbled floor.

Again, she looked to Balthazar for intervention. He gave her a brief glance that showed no signs he knew what the duke was doing to her. Then he turned back to Lady Giselle.

Katerina put the rest of her roll on her plate and moved her hand to her lap, onto to that of the duke's hand on her thigh. She pushed slightly for him to remove his fingers, but he didn't hurry to comply.

Her cheeks heated in irritation by the brazen way he pretended to use her leg as support. Except, he prolonged the touch, sliding it higher, causing her to fight the pleasurable sensations he created in her loins. Damp and hot between her legs, she avoided looking at him when he sat upright and his fingers slipped off her leg.

Another course to their meal was served.

"Herring, my favorite," Giselle commented a little too zealously.

"Ah, something we have in common," Balthazar exclaimed. "Herring is my favorite as well."

Katerina arched a brow. It was the first she heard of her brother's love of fish. He was a meat and potatoes sort of man.

"And he also loves shrimp," Katerina teased, knowing he hated the seafood delicacy.

"Oh, I don't like shrimp myself. I feel as if I'm eating someone's little babies." Giselle flaked off a piece of fish with her fork and put it in her mouth.

"Well we won't have any shrimp on this table tonight," Balthazar declared.

"Hmmm, and I was beginning to like the idea of having a nice dish of chilled shrimp." Katerina turned her gaze to Giselle. "The nice plump ones with the big eyes."

Katerina made the girl cringe on purpose and ignored her brother's reprimanding stare. She turned her attention to the duke.

"Do you have a dislike we should know about, Your Grace? I wouldn't want you to suffer some dreadful illness."

"I'll eat dirt if it's served."

"Don't let him fool you, Your Highness. Dax detests—"

The duke gave his sister a stern look.

Katerina suppressed her amusement. "Do tell us, Lady Giselle."

She couldn't think of anything more exciting than learning what the duke disliked.

"Giselle." The duke's tone stopped Giselle from answering.

"Oh please," Katerina encouraged with a stretch of her hand over the table toward Giselle. "I simply must know."

"If Dax doesn't wish me to say—"

"It cannot be so bad," Balthazar interjected. "I loathe shrimp myself. What should he care if we know of his dislike?"

"I don't like crowberry iced pudding." The duke divulged the answer, heroically relieving his sister of the task.

"Not like iced pudding." Balthazar laughed. "How can you not like the delectable dish?"

"He doesn't like anything having to do with ice or snow or cold," Giselle quietly added. Her expression told the tale of guilt.

The duke's penetrating look made Katerina feel like a villain and she sought to make amends.

"Why Lady Giselle, how good of you to inform me. I detest crowberry iced pudding as well." Katerina waved a servant forward. "I wish to cancel the serving of iced pudding for the duke and myself."

“Yes, Your Highness.” The servant bowed and hurried away.

Giselle appeared as pleased as Balthazar. The duke even gave Katerina a simple approving nod of his head. She had, however, wished for his smile.

They spent the remainder of time during the meal on trivial talk of weather, foreign affairs and personal interests. The duke’s disposition mellowed and Katerina absorbed every tidbit she could from his anecdotes. The dinner moved along, slow in some instances. Once it concluded, Katerina experienced a serene contentment with the duke and his sister’s company, something she hadn’t expected when the meal started.

After the duke rose from his seat with a bow to the prince, Katerina worried the evening had ended too soon. She searched for something she might add to the conversation to keep him longer, but it appeared they’d covered a great deal already and she had nothing left.

“My sister is a very good conversationalist, Your Highness,” the duke told Balthazar. “If you’d please, I should like to excuse myself and hope to have the princess show me around your magnificent palace.”

“Yes.” Balthazar stood and hurried around to pull out Katerina’s chair. “What a splendid idea. She’d be delighted to give you a tour. We have some superb artifacts from the Orient and there is the great hall lined with—”

“Your Highness,” Katerina hissed low, glaring at her brother. “I think he gets the idea you wish us gone.”

“I’m sorry. I didn’t mean you should rush off. It was the duke’s desire for your company that—”

“He aspires to see the palace and for me to be his guide.” She didn’t mean to sound ungrateful for the duke’s reason to have her go along.

"Kat," her brother chastised.

"If I may add, Princess." The duke waited for her to turn her gaze toward him. "I used the ploy of seeing the palace only to spend time with you."

She had enjoyed the duke's easy manner at supper, yet she wanted to scream her refusal to be escorted into some dark corner. Her emotions had the better of her. She didn't want him to leave, except she feared what might transpire if they were alone.

Katerina slowly rose from her chair and decided she'd simply walk out of the room with him. Once they were out of sight of Balthazar, she'd feign a headache and flee to her chambers.

She took hold of the arm the duke offered. To all appearances, she went willingly. She considered what he would do when she decided to leave him standing alone in the corridor. She had guards to prevent him from following her if she so ordered it. Then there was the fact he had been invited for an overnight stay. She didn't particularly like the idea of imprisoning herself in her room, but it would keep her out of the duke's reach.

Katerina had it all decided as they left the dining hall. Balthazar could court Giselle right to the altar and she'd stay in her room until the duke's departure.

The corridor had the lingering scent of rose hanging above the door lintels. She loved roses. They eased her headaches when she sat in her bath infused with the oils. Now they calmed her.

"It's not iced pudding I don't like," the duke informed her as they started their stroll.

Katerina stopped and looked at him. His confession startled her and the idea of departing waned in favor of knowing why he lied at dinner.

"I gave up my ice pudding for you to hide your dislike of something else?"

In the amber glow of a chandelier, a halo of light softened the duke's features. Not a trace of amusement showed on his face. It was disconcerting not knowing if he teased her, until his eyes twinkled and he smiled.

Chapter Thirteen

Dax wished to pare down his lies. He'd already told too many and found it hard to keep them straight.

The corners of the princess's mouth drew up in a beautiful smile. And her laughter—her expressed delight erased the contrariness she had clung to in the past.

He clasped his hands behind his back, unsure what he found prettiest about her—the adamant way she kept up her appearance of disliking him or the ease in which he lured her out of her distrust. Her musical voice, twirling in his head, proved one thing, no one could ever misjudge Princess Katerina of Alluvia more than he had.

Huge portraits lined the walls. Dax turned from her to look at the face of an ancestor she probably never knew.

"My grandfather, the Marquis of Elbian and the Queen of Elbian's consort," she presented. "Now are you going to tell me what food you don't like to eat?"

"And this silly looking fellow?" He moved to another portrait.

"My mother's brother, Prince Duane of Elbian. I'd really like to know what you don't like."

Dax shuffled along to the next portrait. "This gentleman resembles you. Though, he does appear much more hoity-toity." He chuckled. "How is it you're related?"

"My eldest brother." Her voice went quiet. "Prince Lawrence died five years ago."

Dax spun to find her distressed. He picked up her hand and rubbed a thumb over her fingers.

"I was teasing you about the iced pudding. I really don't like the stuff."

"Nor anything cold?"

"Oh, I suppose there are some things enjoyable."

A tear dripped from her lower lid and he wiped it away. "I might not appreciate the beauty of snow, but I've always found it enjoyable to eat."

Her smile eradicated the heaviness from his heart. The blunder he'd made trying to distract her by jest of her family was dismissed by the return of the light mood. Dax lifted her gloved hand. His need to see, to feel her warm fingers, grew and he clenched the tip of one and slid his teeth to the point to jerk it from the finger. Each one he did the same way.

Katerina appeared spellbound by his actions and he continued the slow removal of her glove. Once the item loosened, he tugged it off and slipped it in his jacket pocket.

"Forgive my insensitivity to your loss, Your Highness."

No shield of cloth protected her from his lips. Turning her hand over, he pressed a kiss to the heart of her warm, moist palm. Her shiver was distinct and the sound of excitement clear in the little noise she made. With the back of his finger, he removed a few more tears from her flushed cheeks. The dampness of her smooth skin drew him closer. The transparency of her emotions led his soul on a quest to truly know her.

"Thank you." Her sweet breath incited his blood.

He slipped an arm around her waist. "Am I too close?"

She shook her head slightly.

"Forgive me for my tease?"

Her gaze lowered. "You didn't know." The whispery soft sound caressed his thoughts.

"It was ill-mannered of me to have made any humorous comment about your family, whether alive or not. Now tell me I'm forgiven or I shall depart your castle tonight in disgrace."

Her wet-spiked lashes flipped up.

"You're forgiven."

Give a little, take a little—his goal was to keep Katerina Romanoff off guard and interested in everything he said or did.

Her luscious wine-stained lips attracted him like nothing before. He'd kissed women and had affairs driven by lust, but never had he wanted something more from a relationship.

Dax wanted privacy, the kind for making love to a princess. Trusting she'd take him there on her own, he folded her delicate fingers around his arm.

"Tell me of the others." He walked her along and they stopped at another portrait.

"This is my uncle, Prince Talbot of Alluvia, but he prefers to go by Lord Talbot of Elbian. He is my father's brother and they had a falling out a long time ago that made him refuse to use his true title."

"Yes, I've met him," he said on the chance she had witnessed them talking at the ball. "As a matter of fact I spoke to him briefly last night."

Dax carelessly played with the lace of her sleeve's cuff as they moved on.

"He's one of only a few members left of the Romanoff bloodline who has a portrait in the castle."

"Where is one of you and the prince?" He smoothed his strokes over her velvety knuckles.

"In the throne room." She pointed to the large set of oak doors at the end of the corridor where two guards stood at attention.

"I should like to see them."

Dax walked her there and they didn't have to wait to instruct the guards. The men automatically opened the massive barrier for them.

A plum carpet-runner stretched the length of the room. It rippled up over the dozen steps to a raised floor much like that of the dais in the ballroom. Only this one was more like another level of the room, spanning the whole width, instead of a semicircle in just the middle.

Dax ignored the two new guards posted near the wall, behind and on either side of the single high-backed chair. The ornate wood, embellished with jewels and upholstered in a lighter shade of purple velvet than the carpet, appeared stiff. He let go of the princess's hand and bounded up the steps.

"Looks uncomfortable." He examined the chair, rubbing a hand over his chin.

"Extremely hard on the backside for any length of time."

Dax turned and faced her. He sat and watched her eyes widen. He'd never been very proper in following the royal code of ethics. The placement of his ass on the throne of Alluvia should have had the guards jumping down his throat. However, they were nicely held at bay by the princess and the command of her ever-ready hand. One flick of it kept them away, leaving him safe to ease back in the seat without the fear of his beheading.

"I don't think anyone has ever sat in that chair who wasn't an Alluvian." Her fascination with him glowed in her eyes and brought her forward.

His daring impertinence crossed a line. Although risky, he knew she needed adventure or at least a surprise now and then.

"Bring me a chair," she ordered a guard.

From a row of four equally uncomfortable chairs near the back by the wall, the guard strained to lift one. He hurried forward the best he could and sat it next to the throne chair.

"Both of you wait outside," she instructed the guards, then sat on the edge of the seat.

"How does one sit in this thing for more than five minutes?" Dax tried leaning back.

"With trained stamina." She smiled.

He stood and stared at it. "I would have something a bit more comfortable made if I were to hold court here."

"No you wouldn't. A king is not to be relaxed or he becomes careless in all his thoughts."

Dax got up and took her hand to pull her from her seat.

"Show me how it is you could look at ease on such a piece of furniture."

"Would I, say, be on display for the court?" She adjusted her position and sat with the prim, straight-backed pose that came naturally to her. "Or, am I amongst family and overseeing an argument?" She pulled her feet up and smiled.

"I see your family has a gift for appearing to enjoy the seat, because I don't believe I could ever display relaxation as well as you."

He placed his hands on the wide arms of the chair and leaned close to her face. She held steady in all except the shift of her gaze.

"Do you also pretend to enjoy the place of power, Princess?"

Chapter Fourteen

Katerina gasped and blinked. She drew back, even though she wanted him to kiss her so badly it hurt to be near his lips. He suggested she might be a pretentious ruler, acting only for the sake of appearance to cultivate the populace into liking her.

The room took on a smallness she felt trapped in with the duke. He leaned closer, not allowing her a retreat. The heat of his body enveloped her and she perspired. His face neared until his nose almost touched hers. She gripped the arms of the chair tighter. Her heart anxiously pounded with a little apprehension and a mild excitement.

"I think y-you...misjudge me," she stammered.

"Do I? How?"

"You assume I rule people to serve me. However, I serve them through the power the throne gives me."

Her gaze dropped to his mouth and his followed to hers.

"I'd never abuse my position," she whispered.

The sexy lines at the corners of the duke's mouth intrigued her. Close enough to kiss, her lips parted in anticipation. He did nothing and it occurred to her she could order him to press his mouth to hers. Unfortunately, she had grown to know his habits and, for torture, he would disobey the command.

"I dare say I have offended you by my bluntness, Your Highness." He stood and the room expanded. "Shall I leave?"

"No. I mean—" She stood ready for him to take his leave of her. "Do as you wish."

She never felt such distance separate her from anything as that of the duke moving out of reach. He walked several paces and turned, coming back at her with a conquering smile that made her knees rattle. He gripped her arms with the steely length of his fingers. Pulling, not hard, but swift, he left her the choice to fight the presumptuous hold or surrender.

Katerina relinquished command of her body. She leaned against the duke's firm chest and waited for him to proceed.

"I wish to kiss you, Princess."

His fingers skated over her cheek to the side of her head. She didn't speak, move or answer for fear he'd withdraw.

"With your permission, of course."

She couldn't believe he asked when he'd taken what he wanted the night before.

Katerina stared into the depths of his gaze. The magnificence of his boldness hypnotized her. She didn't want to think of anything but what his mouth would do to her senses.

Emotions had run high in recent weeks. The impending disposition of her father's will required actions foreign to her. If the duke hadn't said he had no wish to court her, she could very well see herself asking him to marry her. Perhaps they would get along. Maybe they'd bicker endlessly. Except the attraction to him pushed her into the dangerous territory of taking chances even though he had the power to hurt her with his rejection.

Lowering her eyes, she let her lashes lay on her cheeks as a sign of resignation and acceptance.

"I do believe that is a yes." He gave a soft laugh—a mockery of her submissiveness.

Before she protested his abuse of her willingness, his mouth slanted across hers and pressed firmly.

Katerina sighed with relief.

The duke's tongue slid over hers and the slippery wetness of his inspection tickled every fiber in her. She slackened her stance, encouraging his arms to tighten and hold her.

His mouth moved, slowly sucking and teasing her with gentle nibbles. The embrace of his strong arms didn't budge, while she slid her hands all over his hard back, enjoying the feel of his muscles beneath his clothes. She was delighted by the way his mouth moved from hers a smidge and attached again. Her small hum of pleasure was meant to encourage him, yet he abruptly ended the kiss. He stepped back, releasing her.

"Thank you, Princess, just the thing a man needs before bed."

Stunned, Katerina blindly raised her arm and tugged a bell to summon the guards outside the room. She believed he wanted to make love to her and the coldness of his words swept a disappointing chill through the very limbs he heated with his kiss. The lust in his gaze, the teasing way he touched her were sensations she enjoyed.

"Guards, please show His Grace to the guest chambers in the east wing," she instructed when they entered. "He and his sister will be staying with us."

Katerina stood inflexibly straight with her chin held high and her hands at her sides. She worked extra hard at maintaining her indifference—refusing to speak to him again.

"Goodnight, Princess."

Katerina's kiss-puckered mouth had Dax flustered. Her innocence showed she didn't give her favors easily and he would have trouble resisting her inexperience if he remained. While he found pride in the accomplishment of breaking her will, he suffered a great humility. To have the princess melting and melding into his embrace had a profound effect on his trembling heart. Even though he would have liked to indulge in the pleasures of her kiss, he had to leave her wanting.

Katerina's blank face gave him no hint at what she felt. Hoping he hadn't ruined his plans for her, Dax jumped down the steps two at a time. He strolled to the door where the guards waited.

"Now if you'll point me to my bedchamber, gentlemen, I think I'll turn in for the night. It has been a rather exhausting week with the traveling, the ball and all those women I entertained on my arm."

Dax glanced over his shoulder at Katerina. She barely breathed let alone allowed her gaze to connect with his. It was a sad moment to have brought her hopes up and then crush them as if she meant nothing to him.

"I suggest you might do with a little sleep yourself, Princess. You look a little rumpled," he said, anticipating some reaction from her.

A statue would seem more alive than she did in her rigid stance.

"Come men, I do need some sleep," Dax told the guards.

He kept contact with the princess's stare. At the exit, he bowed to her.

"Pleasant dreams, Your Highness." The door closed and the echo drummed along the corridor.

Dax should have been happy with his accomplishment. He had shown the princess a taste of something she couldn't command. With her eating out of his hand for every morsel of affection she thought she could entice, he was in control of the situation.

Nevertheless, with his heart involved, he had trouble rejoicing at the prospect of her suffering.

Stepping a few feet away, he turned, recalling the mention of a wardrobe from which he might get fresh clothes.

"Just a moment men. I forgot something I need to ask the princess."

Opening the door a little to stick his head in, he saw Katerina drop to the floor. With her arm folded on the flat cushion of the throne, she put her head down. Her sniffled sob ricocheted around the room and stabbed him. He wanted her off guard with her feelings toward him, but he hadn't wanted her to be genuinely upset.

"I'll ask tomorrow," he whispered to the guards and pulled the door closed.

Dax felt ill about the way he had hurt Katerina's feelings. Yet he couldn't tell her the truth of why he treated her shabbily. His country's welfare had to stay at the forefront of his thoughts and his actions. There wasn't room for his emotional guilt.

Chapter Fifteen

Katerina tossed and turned throughout the night. Nightmares crept into her dreams.

Her uncle, Lord Talbot, mercilessly gripped her arms behind the throne chair. She twisted to break free. She shook from tiny explosions she was made to endure by another man she couldn't see.

Her body ached in the awkward position. Her arms burned from the strain as Lord Talbot kept them wrenched back. Aside from her discomfort, she shuddered from a feathering sensation. She wished she could open her eyes and find the explanation.

Stefan had touched her with the adoring smacks of his tongue. Her heart stopped, her lungs seized. She sat on the throne chair naked. She wore nothing at all except the man's head between her legs. She knew it was a man's head, but she couldn't look to be sure.

"I wish to kiss you." The duke's voice spoke the plea instead of Stefan's.

"Yes," she answered. "Yes please!"

Her mouth hadn't been his goal. His head went down and she inhaled sharply. He sucked hard on her cunt, parting and prodding the inner lips with sweet kisses.

"Are you frigid, Princess? I think not from this vantage point."

She lifted her hips to the thrusting tongue, dipping and swirling inside her.

"Then, maybe Lord Talbot has a different idea."

Her uncle's face came down close to hers. His wicked smile made her sick. He licked her cheek and in a panic, she kicked at the duke.

"Let me go," she demanded.

"Relax, Your Highness."

The duke stretched her legs wider. He destroyed the muscles in her thighs. They didn't appreciate the position or the force. The pounding of her heart came faster and she moaned with the intense orgasm forming in the background of all her other sensations.

"Katerina, are you awake?" Balthazar shouted.

She bolted upright on the bed. Her fingers still lay tucked between her legs, wet from the gushing warm liquid of her dreaming nightmare. One kiss from the duke, and he managed to find a place in the nightly visions plaguing her.

With the stir of cool morning air, fine beads of perspiration chilled her. The coal fire in the grate had gone out because she had dismissed her personal maid.

Katerina placed her feet over the side of the bed and touched the cold floor with ten protesting toes that curled against the icy wood.

"Katerina." Balthazar rapped on the door again and her hand covered her pounding heartbeat.

"Just a minute." She reached for her slippers.

Her robe lay right where she left it draped over the footboard. Her headache had returned, leaving her barely capable of moving. Putting on the robe became a time-consuming chore. She slid her arms into the heavy brocade sleeves.

"Kat?"

She glanced in the mirror. Before the dreams or the nightmares, she had cried herself to sleep. She had no reason why the duke affected her the way he did.

"Please, Balthazar, just go away for a little while." If she opened the door he'd not leave without questioning her red-rimmed eyes.

"Are you all right?"

"Of course."

"I saw your light on from under the door."

"It's my headache again. I fell asleep without turning down the lamp."

"I'll check on you in a little while, then."

"No. If I'm asleep, you'll only disturb me. It's the middle of the night. I'll be fine."

She sat at her dressing table and stared in the mirror. She wasn't old and yet her face appeared drained. Headaches, nightmares and a kingdom to save were diseases eating away her youth. She rose, not wishing to dwell on what she couldn't change. Going to the door, she eased it open and checked to make sure the hall was empty. The usual guards were in position at the end of the long runner of dyed-wool carpet, but no one else.

It wasn't common for her to walk the corridors of the palace without dressing first. Yet, not a sentry batted an eye as she floated along the passages. She passed guards stationed. There to protect the royal family, they had become fixtures and she hardly took notice of them.

She went directly to the throne room—a place of power. She gathered strength with recollections of her father ruling from that seat. He never wavered in anyone's presence and when she had asked, he said that weakness was a ruler's duty to hide.

Katerina observed the two men posted back behind the throne chair. Like a staged production, they were neatly attired and at attention. It made her wonder if they got bored and relaxed against the wall when no one was in the room. Maybe they weren't needed at night, but tradition had a way of making some habits stick. When her ancestors had enemies they required many guards.

She sat on the chair and for a brief second, smiled. It was the hardest piece of furniture in the palace. Curling her legs up, she held her knees and thought about her brother. She wondered how soon he'd ask Giselle to marry him.

Their Uncle Talbot's presence at the ball showed how closely he watched them. He circled the palace like a vulture for what he considered his rightful place on the throne. It was a cruel world that marriage had to be for anything other than love.

"Princess?"

Katerina lifted her head. She hadn't expected to see the duke. The guards shouldn't have let him in and she found it highly presumptuous of them to think because she let him sit on the throne he could come and go as he pleased.

By chance she looked at one guard. The two in the room were different than earlier. At midnight there would have been a changing of the guard throughout the palace. She thought of Stefan and how she liked him. When her father caught wind of her flirtation with the page and later a guard, they were dismissed from duty. She never saw Stefan again and the guard had been pure rumor, nothing more.

"Excuse my interruption." The duke gave the lowest bow she'd seen from him and he proceeded to back out the door.

"Wait." Katerina ran down the steps to him. "Is there something I can do for you?"

Too eagerly the words came out and she couldn't take them back.

"Ah, Princess, what an open invitation you offer. However, I have no need for your company in my bed tonight, maybe another time."

"How dare you." She slapped his cheek and waited for some retort. Some wonderfully wicked response.

He had to say something, do something to her, another insolent comment or lewd suggestion, whatever, as long as he ended it by kissing her. She didn't want to think how much he made her desire his brash ways, but she relished his domination over her senses. The need to have him arouse her, as he did in her dreams, led the way for the pack of other wild thoughts tumbling in her mind. He said he didn't need her in his bed, God how she wanted him in hers.

Even though the duke's hair was slightly rumpled, he still wore the same clothes and she assumed he hadn't slept. His disheveled appearance didn't detract from his good looks but rather enhanced his attractiveness. His hand raked through the locks, stirring them into a new order. After which, his hand smoothed over the red imprint on his skin. He smiled and gave her a tilt of his head, conceding her right to reprimand him.

"Goodnight, my Princess." He backed completely from the room, leaving her in a wake of his scent.

Katerina let out a shriek of pure frustration. The guards in the room hurried down from the dais. She couldn't see the ones in the corridor.

"Bring him back here." She pointed at the door opening with the command. "Bring him in here and leave us alone."

Chapter Sixteen

Prepared for the princess to do something, her scream had been the least of Dax's worries. When the doors opened, he imagined her storming out, ordering the guards to shoot him on the spot.

Beyond the guards approaching him, the princess stood regally and more radiant than the fiery lights of the Aurora Borealis.

He surrendered before they grabbed him.

"I'll go peacefully to her wrath."

Then giving a brush of his hand over his head and a jerk to smooth down his jacket, he walked through the open doorway. Entering, straightening his cravat with a firm tug, he advanced until the doors slammed shut. Dax stopped and looked behind to see the guards closing him off from their protection.

"So, do you wish to speak to me or do you do your own beheading?"

Her chest heaved and before he could imagine her hitting him again, she flew at him, and pressed her lips to his. She was straightforward with her desires and he gave an equal share of his.

She coiled her arms around him, seeking his full attention. His teasing lick followed the rim of her mouth. She met him in the center with a flick of her tongue. The heat of their breath mingled, blended and sealed between them as he closed the gap.

Holding her firmly to him, caressing the length of her back, he felt every shudder and tremble her body made. He nipped and tugged at her bottom lip, drawing away and replanting his kiss.

"Is this my punishment?" he whispered upon parting from her heated gasp.

"Yes, dammit." She claimed his mouth again.

Dax savored the aggressive movement. Allowing her free reign, he enjoyed her exploratory verve as she kissed outside the bounds of his lips. She held the back of his head with the tips of her fingers pressing hard.

Her other arm slid around him tighter, grasping the jacket in the center of his spine. He squeezed Katerina's whole body to him, giving up all thought of letting her go.

Tired of the diversions he forced her to endure, the serious game of seduction took a unique turn, spelling success for him. In his arms, by her own doing, Princess Katerina became his. Even though he brutally tried to make her hate him, she clung to his hungering soul. He'd not fail in his plot against her.

"Why, Princess?" He held her face and stared into her lovely eyes.

The watery gaze darted inquisitively over his face. She was the conqueror for the moment.

"Why what?" As usual, her nervousness intrigued him.

"Why did you have to be so damned beautiful?" He rushed another deeper kiss into her panting breath.

Dax undid the tie to her heavy robe. He slid his hands beneath, taking in the curve of her hips. Her warm body wiggled closer. He pushed his palms flat over her ribs. One hand took the route of encircling her small waist. His other hand captured the fullness of her rounded breast.

He drew his head back.

"Don't stop."

"I didn't plan to, but I was checking to be sure you're all right with this."

She nodded and he pressed his mouth against her smiling one.

She whimpered as he rolled his thumb over the tip of her breast. Softly peaked, the tip hardened with his persuasive stroke. The pearl-shaped nipple, plump and succulent, demanded his kisses. Only he couldn't detach from her lips. She had an adoring purr and he ate up every morsel of sweet saliva in her mouth. He'd hated the short kiss from earlier. This was what he preferred all along.

While kissing, he spread his legs and allowed her lower region to fit against him. Just as the night of the ball, she pressed her sex to the muscle of his thigh. This time she forced herself upon him with a severe urgency. His cock wouldn't hold out long against her taunting body rubbing him.

Dax left the center of her mouth for the creased corner.

"Easy, beautiful." He used a hand to shift her off his erection.

The upturn of her seductive smile lured him to the heat of her blushing cheek.

He hadn't noticed her fingers at the cravat until her nails scratched at his skin beneath. She worked the silken cloth loose and he dropped his head back for her kisses along his jaw and into the dampness of his neck. His swallow rushed his Adam's apple up and down, bumping over her lips coasting to the hollow. He pulled the cloth away, entangling her wrist. Twirling her around, Dax pushed her back to a pillar. Not one of the wide supports of the room, but a narrow and smooth pylon of granite meant to decorate the room with almost a dozen others. It suited his need of tying up the princess.

Would she appreciate how her body would sing in praise of passive bondage? The warmed female, feral and willing to risk his rejection, looked primed to be defiled in the best of ways.

Dax swung the silk around the column and looped it over her other wrist.

"What are you doing?" Her eyes held a moment of panic.

"I'm going to kiss you from head to toe."

"No."

"Oh yes, definitely yes." He held the loops of the white scarf so she was restrained. "You've been begging me to taste every ounce of your flesh."

"I've not." She twisted with the denial.

"Haven't you, Princess?" He wrapped the ends of the scarf around his wrists and held them.

She could easily unwind the thin material from her arms. He had no real control other than the playful one he let her imagine.

"Please." The word made no genuine demand.

"It will be my pleasure to please you." He kissed under her jaw and worked the robe off her shoulders. Her sable tresses were loosely fitted into a plait he tugged free of the binding ribbon. "I love your hair. The fragrance, texture and most especially how it will look draping your pert nipples."

"Someone will come," she gasped when he unbuttoned her nightgown and kissed the fabric away from her shoulder. Her breasts jiggled with her quivering plea for him to stop.

Once his tongue swirled her dusky areola, she hushed. He sucked in the dark ripened tip through the nightgown. The princess's silky flesh had a delicious flavor. She purred with an unruffled, calm sound. It pleased all his senses and drew his cock to attention. He wanted inside her and he wanted there fast.

Dax lifted and smiled.

"Soon, my beautiful Princess, very soon I'll make you come, into my hand, onto my tongue, and over my cock. I'll taste your sweet spending and drink in your wracking sobs of ecstasy. When I'm done, you'll not care if the entire palace watches. Your rapture will be that intense."

Her eyes danced in a blend of delight and anxiety. Did she suspect something of which he spoke would hurt her?

Dax kissed her soft lips with reserve, allowing her time to relax. He required her desperate, to surrender all her will to him. He aimed to have every sweet kiss of hers blend with a tantalizing erotic need for more.

His kiss deepened and he felt her tug the binds preventing her from throwing her arms around his neck as she had done before. The restriction had to be a very hard thing for her. A life of privilege allowed for half of what a person wanted. Orders, commands and directives never equaled the private dreams, wishes or needs.

"Please, Your Grace."

"Oh, my sweet princess, I've plans. You can't imagine how I can please you."

"But..."

He drowned her protest with another kiss.

Chapter Seventeen

Katerina returned the duke's kiss with urgency. The sensations she experienced from the openness of the room tightened her nipples with anxiousness. Guards stood outside the room. They'd not enter, but her brother might if he checked on her again and didn't get her to answer.

"We must stop," she pleaded. "Balthazar could come in here."

The duke stopped his kisses upon her neck.

"Take a chance, Princess. Live dangerously."

Her skin quivered beneath his hot breath. His scent strengthened with his sweat and she liked it.

"Do you really want me to stop?" His fingers rubbed the tip of her breast as he talked.

"No."

He opened his mouth wider and latched his teeth onto her flesh while sealing her skin with his lips. Sucking hard with a fierce pull to her jugular, he caressed the artery, stimulating the pressure point until she weakened.

He released before she fainted.

Katerina rolled her head from one side to the other, moaning with pleasure as he attacked a fresh place on her neck.

"I've marked you, Princess." He licked over the tender spot.

"Mmmm, yes," she submitted.

He did more and she thrived with the ardent ways he sucked on her body. Clawing his arm, his waist, and gripping the seat of his trousers, she drew him against her. Her robe and nightgown hung around her elbows, trapped by his ties. The fact the very clothes she wore also assisted in giving him a new restraint for her movements, didn't matter.

The duke left her neck and lowered.

"Oh God," she breathed.

His osculation traveled to her chest. The diaphanous cloth covering her breasts became nothing but a wet piece of fabric he suckled with her nipple, until he nudged the cloth away.

"Duke," she panted.

"Call me Dax."

Katerina pressed her breast to his mouth and his teeth pinched her nipple in a tender vise. She arched with fervent excitement.

The tease of heated air from his nostrils turned her in ways she couldn't control. She writhed with erotic tension.

"Dax," she groaned.

The informality of calling him by name seemed stranger than what she let him do to her.

He moved to her other breast and she nearly fainted at the nip he took to the sensitized tip.

"You've delightful nipples, Princess, tender, supple and plump."

She had no words to respond. Wet from the flux of her heated pores, she dripped with perspiration.

"And your breasts are firm, silky and delicious." He nuzzled the underside with his nose, kissing and licking her skin in gentle sweeps. His attentiveness moved her beyond her fantasies.

Katerina's dreams had never been as vivid.

The duke sank to his knees. It gave her arms freedom since his hands gripped her thighs instead of the scarf. She balanced herself by putting hands on his shoulders as he lifted her nightgown. Her pussy clenched—knowing what came next. Or so she thought, until his lips touched the flatness of her belly. Her muscles shrank from the ticklish flick of his tongue. She could no longer suppress a giggle.

"You like that, I see." He licked her again.

His tongue circled and spiraled inward, dipping into her navel and retreating.

"Yes." She clutched his shoulders tighter.

He brushed the nightgown aside and kissed along the fringes of her sex. Katerina's intense passion for this man created new and intriguing feelings. She offered up the center of her being, thrusting her hips forward in hopes he'd find the sweet spot of her desire.

"Relax, Princess, I'm far from giving you the pleasure that you seek." His breathless voice traveled down.

When he said he'd kiss her from head to toe, she'd thought metaphorically, not literally.

"Oh!" she squeaked as the kisses fell over her knee and then behind.

Her insides lurched with a swift jolt. The duke's fingers snuck in to play with her drenched pussy and gathered up all her wild thoughts. His thumb swept open the slit and he fondled the inner lips with careless pauses.

"Please." She reached for his head.

No dream gave her what Dax did—not since Stefan's sweet young mouth had sucked on her. She never thought she'd have such a real experience again.

Dax's finger penetrated the entrance and Katerina jerked. Her insides exploded in a tiny quake. Her shudders didn't stop him from pumping and plunging his fingers, one, then two at a time, into her core.

Deeper and deeper he went, hitting an area that heightened her orgasm.

"Dax, please," she cried.

"Please what? Tell me what you want." He sucked on her belly while his hand worked inside her.

"Please, don't stop."

The cool column she aligned her spine with did nothing to alleviate the concentrated heat.

"You taste delicious." His kisses pressed into her mound.

And then Dax shoved his tongue into the same channel his fingers once filled. With dynamic vigor, he took her body on a ride over a rainbow of emotions and sensations. Like a kaleidoscope, the colors behind her shut eyes showed her the beauty of a man's seduction.

The glorious aggression of his mouth inflamed her pussy. He soothed the tender flesh with wet, cooling licks. His groan echoed inside her and she strained to watch him lap at her swollen clit. All she saw was his head full of black hair.

"Oh no," she gasped. "Yes."

The sensations of the male tongue, slick and coarse, reminded her it had been a long time—a very long time—since Stefan lapped at her in the same fashion. He had given her an orgasm, but Dax gave her passion. Rough, irregular and stimulating, he drove her senses into an erogenous splendor of no comparison.

Katerina gave a thought to Dax's cock. Was it large? Would he have as much energy driving it into her as he did his tongue? God, she was a virgin in the worst way. She wanted a man to make love to her and she feared it for the painful stories she'd heard over the years.

Katerina reached the apex of her climax. Her body flushed, her breasts swelled and her insides contracted.

His breath, a dragon's inferno, streamed out of his nostrils, sending uncontrollable shivers along the same routes as her fired veins. She felt faint with ecstasy, weak with release and euphorically enamored. Her buried sexual obsession lay in reserve for the right man and she had him within reach.

She stretched out her arm and learned Dax had completely released the scarf limiting movement of her hands. Burying her fingers in his hair, she guided, controlled and urged him to purge her sex of the maddening ache. Rocking her hips to his thrusting tongue, she screamed in the throes of pure blissful abandon.

With the cries came a thud at the door.

Dax rose up and pulled her around the column. He blocked her from view of the intruder.

Katerina's nightgown dropped to cover her legs, yet the rest of her clothing hung on her bent elbows until she jerked them up. A strange dizziness blurred her vision and she leaned her head back against the column.

"Your Highness, we heard a scream," a guard said.

Her mouth opened and she couldn't speak. The worst kind of mortification locked her jaw and her hand squeezed Dax's arm. Tears fell to her cheeks. Her headache came on strong and immobilizing. Her legs, thighs and everything inside shook violently.

"The princess tripped and she bumped the column with an elbow," Dax explained with a little chuckle. "You know how painful that funny bone can be."

"Princess?" The guard questioned the validity of the duke's story as well he should.

"You're dismissed," her shaky voice managed.

The door made a resounding clunk as it shut.

"We came close to exposing you to some of the palace guards." Dax laughed, turning around. "However, I've the impression you've done this before."

Blackness closed in on Katerina.

She barely caught a glimpse of Dax's smile, before she closed her eyes and sank into the dark.

Dax almost missed grabbing the princess as she collapsed. He had been with women enough times to think he'd seen everything. With a shot of masculine pride, he cradled her against him to fix her robe around her. He had to forgo the sash and scooped her up.

"Dear one." He kissed her brow. "You do a man's heart good."

Dax walked to the door, boldly opened it and hoped the guards believed she fell asleep.

"Show me to Katerina's room," he ordered firmly, putting forth his most commanding tone.

There was no hesitation and he followed them. He thought using her name might prove helpful. After all, the men weren't morons. They would have suspected all along the princess and he were having an affair.

Another guard at the door to her chambers was not impressed by Dax's unheard of appearance with the princess snuggled against him.

"What has happened?" the guard asked opening the door.

"Shush man, she fell asleep."

"It's those dreadful headaches. She doesn't get much sleep as of late."

Dax looked at the man and his wizened face. He shook free the idea he might be one of her lovers.

"She has them often?"

"They started when her mother died. Since her father's passing, I can say I've hardly seen her without a headache."

"Leave us, now. Katerina asked I stay awhile if she should fall asleep."

The guard gave him a distrustful stare.

"Maybe I should disturb her sleep so she can tell you herself to leave." Dax stared at the man.

"That won't be necessary, Your Grace. If you should need me, I'll be outside."

"And your name?"

"Phillip."

"Since you've offered assistance, my mother had a remedy for such afflictions. As soon as possible, see if you can get me a bowl of ice water filled with red rose petals. It must be ice, not simply cold water, and I'll need her lady's maid."

"Right away, Your Grace."

Dax put Katerina on the bed. He fixed her nightgown and tied her robe.

"I know you'd rather be presentable in something else for when your lady's maid comes for my instructions, but alas, I haven't time to torture myself with your lovely body by dressing you."

He touched the dappled marks of purple on her ivory neck. All paled in comparison to the first love bite. He moved around the bed, fixing her rumpled covers. It appeared she'd been struggling with them through the night. He noted her preference for the color violet. Everything in the room was a milky purple.

The tap at the door came all too soon and he bent over Katerina.

"Things will be difficult for you, dear one. There are a great number of things you'll not like that I must do, but I can only hope you have a forgiving nature." He kissed her forehead. "I'll see you in a couple hours and maybe by then I'll have thought of an alternative to my plans for you."

She moaned with a contented mewl. He put one more kiss on her cute nose and went to the door. Not wanting to disturb the princess with conversation, he stood in the corridor with the lady's maid.

"Your Grace." The woman bobbed a quick curtsey.

The guard came behind her with the bowl of ice and roses. "Is this as you wish, Your Grace?"

"Yes." Dax looked at the young woman. "When the princess has an unbearable headache, put your fingers in the ice water until you can't feel your fingers. Then, put the very tips of your fingers against her eyelids, pressing slightly into the upper part of the socket. Avoid touching the part covering the eye itself. Her headache will go away much faster."

Chapter Eighteen

Katerina stood at the window, looking forward to seeing the white winter land, but not the Duke of Maltar. She had questioned her guard, Phillip, to learn the duke only stayed in her room for a short time while waiting for her maid. The cure for a headache he sent with the woman, worked well, maybe too well. A clear mind allowed her to focus on what she had let him do to her only a few hours earlier.

She dreaded seeing Dax again, especially on an outing with others. What would he say or divulge of their quite accidental rendezvous?

She paced the room nervously.

"Throwing myself at him," she moaned.

The duke had gotten under her skin in more ways than she wanted to think about. Yet, she wanted to remember him with the same clarity she used to remember Stefan. She needed a mature man to envision in the sometimes sweet dreams. That His Grace was also in her nightmares scared her. It seemed to omen a bad end for them.

Katerina dismissed the saddening thoughts from her head. She didn't want to think of disaster when her insides soared with happiness.

Stopping to look in the mirror again, she smiled. She hadn't been wrong. Dax wanted her as much as she wanted him.

Her fingers slid down the splash of purple stains on her neck. Mortified to see them, she recalled the way she pleaded for him not to stop anything he did to her. There remained two reasons for not having His Grace ejected from her palace. The anticipation of the duke's hands on her bare skin and the expression on Balthazar's face when he looked at Giselle.

At the knock on her door, Katerina put her robe on. "Come in."

"You're not dressed, yet." Balthazar grabbed her hands and danced her around the room.

"It won't take me long." She held his face and kissed him lightly on his cheek. "You're too happy for this time of the morning."

"Kat, I'm in love." He sung the words and dropped into a chair with her on his lap. "I have never felt this way toward any lady before."

Before she could get away, his hand went to her neck.

"Lady Giselle is quite lovely," she agreed.

"Kat?"

She pushed up from him and stood.

"You have only known her for a short time. Don't you think you might give it a week before professing undying affection?"

"No. Besides, one of us has to be married by the end of the month and I don't see you hurrying to the altar. I didn't even see you considering anyone until...I do believe you have turned Maltar's head." He chuckled.

"It's not as you think." Her lips trembled as she recalled the horrible statement the duke made declaring he had no wish to court her.

"You two seem to have overcome your differences. How shall I say this? Maybe you've been closer than visible?" His fingers swept the collar of her robe aside.

Katerina put a hand over the marks on her neck. Balthazar's teasing made her wonder if Dax would comment on the passion bites as well. She moved behind a dressing screen.

"Should I make an objection—speak to him regarding the virtue of my sister?"

She lifted the gown she had instructed her maid to put out for her. "My virtue is safe. Besides, don't you think it a double-standard if I haven't and you can?" She wiggled the gown into place and smoothed over the pleats and folds of her favorite dress.

"A man expects—"

"Oh don't get me started on what a man expects. If you did, then what of the women you've sullied, Balthazar? What of those woman and the men they finally marry? Men can't have it both ways."

"So then, why haven't you?"

"I'd like to think it's because I have self-respect, but I dare say it's because no man has tried." She looked at her sealskin boots and debated stockings.

"And the duke?"

"I have no intention of looking at him as more than your future brother-in-law." She came out all dressed and Balthazar laughed.

"What? Did I button it up wrong?" She looked in the mirror and fingered the buttons running from her long neck all the way down to the floor. “It’s all in order, none are missing. I look perfect.”

Balthazar continued laugh.

“What is so funny?”

“That’s your favorite gown. You only wear it on special occasions.”

“I don’t find that amusing. I just...just wanted to look nice in front of Lady Giselle.” It sounded dumb and she laughed with him. “Oh, I hope he eats his heart out knowing he can’t have me. Those sparks between the duke and myself would only lead to a dangerous fire, consuming us with complete resentment.”

“At least you admit to having feelings for him.”

“Balthazar, I know you worry as much as I do about what will happen with our situation. Don’t include my personal problems.”

He got up and took her hands. “Kat, you’re my sister. Your troubles become mine by default. You can’t simply shut me out because too much is going on. Now tell me, what crisis are you having difficulty with?”

“I vowed not to let the duke rile me anymore. After you woke me up last night, I took a walk and ran into him.” Her eyes watered with the memory. She couldn’t get past that statement as hard as she tried. “Balthazar, he said he doesn’t want me.”

“You mean what he said at the ball? Kat, a man doesn’t go to all this trouble—” He rubbed a finger along her neck. “Believe me a man just doesn’t leave behind marks like this without great passion and deep feelings for a woman.”

“Really?”

“I see you and Maltar as similar people—headstrong, independent and afraid to let your emotions show.”

"That I can assure you has not been the case. If anything, I've been too emotional."

"If you'd like to know him, then try not to boil over at every vexing thing he says or does."

"That will be hard. He likes to upset me."

"Maybe you make him nervous and he can't help his actions."

"The Duke of Maltar doesn't do anything without motive. He's plotted and planned his advance and retreats, all to torture me."

"Or to gain your undivided attention."

"I don't know what he's up to, but there is something he wants."

"Oh? Like what?"

"A king for his sister."

"Would that be so bad—to want his sister in a suitable marriage?" He walked to her and touched her cheek. "I want the very same for you. Unmarried kings are hard to come by, but dukes are not."

"She at least has a chance. I don't think I'll ever find anyone again."

"Again? So you admit you like him?"

"He's not bad looking and he's definitely not old. That is all I'll credit to his advantage."

"Don't forget he's tall. I do believe that is one of your requirements."

"Yes, impressively so." She smiled.

"Then give him a chance, Kat. Be the sweet, generous, loving girl you are and maybe it'll have an effect on him. Ready?" He picked up her fur coat and grabbed her hand.

"No, but let's get this over with." She liked his exuberance and his optimism.

Give the duke a chance, her brother suggested. She had given the man several in the most intimate ways possible. How or why should she provide him another? She didn't need a vain duke who thought more of his own comforts than hers. Even the last moment she could remember before fainting, he had joked about people seeing her. She wanted a man who doted on her every whim, satisfied all her wishes and treated her royally, as befit her station.

Still, the duke stirred a darker need. His arrogance made her breath come short and ragged as if it might be her last. His touch caused her heart to race. Then there were his eyes. They followed her moves with such longing. He never once glanced at her that she couldn't see he liked what he saw. Her fingers smoothed over the gown. It was sheer vanity to dress in her finest for him or seek his favor by her appearance.

Chapter Nineteen

Giselle bounced anxiously on the edge of the bed. "Hurry, hurry, hurry," she insisted for the hundredth time.

"He's not going to leave without us." Dax yanked his boot on and tucked in the leg of his trousers. "I take it, after I left you two together, all went smoothly?"

"He's adorable. You know he took me up to the tower and showed me the stars. I've never experienced a more magical time." She continued her impatient jostling of the bed as she talked. "Dax, you're taking too long."

"Giselle." He gripped her wrists and stared at her.

"Dax, that hurts." She pulled free.

"Don't fall in love with him, Giselle. He would not love you if he knew who you were and why you're here. I don't want you to fantasize that it's possible."

He turned away, guilty of berating her for the same thing he had been falling victim to since he saw the princess. Everything about Katerina—her strengths and her weaknesses—wove around his deep longing for love.

"Do this, don't do that. All you are is full of orders and instructions. Just because Princess Katerina doesn't like you, don't spoil my fun."

"We have one purpose for this trip."

"I won't forget why we're here. How can I? It doesn't mean I can't have a good time." She shoved his coat sleeves onto his arms. "You would do well to behave nicer to the princess. You've been acting like a complete snob."

"Then I have accomplished what I intended."

"Alienating her?"

"Arousing her curiosity and something harder to resist." Dax jerked the coat into place on his shoulders.

"And what would that be?"

"She needs a husband and she's developed an attraction to me, yet I've led her to believe I'm unavailable."

"How does that help us?"

"She wants me more because she can't have me."

Giselle looked at him, skeptical, but took his arm without voicing the concerns expressed in her eyes.

They walked down the hall and Dax said nothing more to tame her excitement. She knew their mission and he couldn't dictate his sister's emotions any more than he could command his own.

"Ah, there are my most honored guests." Balthazar displayed an ecstatic energy.

Giselle's smile was no less glorious when she aimed it at Balthazar. Dax saw her heart was lost. Too late came his own warning not to fall in love.

Outside the palace walls, in the cold air of the courtyard, stood horses snorting and dancing with anticipation. Dax approached Katerina with caution.

"Good morning, Princess." He held her hand to assist her in mounting the gray gelding. "I hope you slept well."

"Fine, thank you."

Her expression hinted at excitement, while her reply was overshadowed with a disturbing coldness.

He went to the horse he'd ride, a calm Caspian mare.

Dax and Katerina waited quietly for the prince to finish checking Giselle's rigging on the small black mare for the second time. He appeared to be as smitten with Giselle as she with him.

"That looks better, m'lady." The prince placed a hand on her back as she stepped up to the platform to get on the horse. "I wouldn't want you fall."

"Thank you, Your Highness." Giselle glowed.

"Katerina, you and Maltar go ahead. I'll check my saddle also." He gave a sly, excited wink to his sister as if Dax were invisible.

"Very well." Katerina turned her horse away. "I was growing weary of waiting for you to stop fussing anyways."

If he didn't trust the prince's intentions, Dax wouldn't have left Giselle. But as fate had arranged things, the regent needed a wife, and he needed one soon. It was unlikely the prince would do anything indecent to offend Giselle.

Besides, there were four guards with them.

Dax looked over his shoulder, a bit perturbed by the fact there were also four guards coming along with him and the princess. Total privacy seemed elusive. While guards were often looked upon as insignificant fixtures in the day-to-day life of royalty, the things he planned to do with the princess required them to be alone. He had no wish of an audience when he made love to the beautiful woman.

With a snap of her wrist, Katerina tapped her horse lightly on the shoulder with her short riding crop.

"It's a lovely countryside," Dax commented riding up alongside her. "I can imagine it to be equally beautiful in the summer, especially if you're part of the landscape."

A compliment. That was not what she expected after their last encounter. The way he bounced between mean and nice, she assumed he'd hold some grudge against her for their morning affair.

This pleasantness put her on the defensive for something more severe he'd spring on her later. She'd not let him lull her into a false sense of security.

"Everything is breathtaking, regardless of whether I'm here or not." His frown pushed her to add. "The meadows are very colorful in the summer with wildflowers."

"My perfect time of year."

"Do you detest the winter's cold that much?"

"I find snow a nuisance in getting around without difficulty, yes. But it's the shortage of food for the poor, coal or wood for our heat, and shelter for those that have little that bother me."

She looked at him with questions forming.

"Compassion, my princess. I am flawed in that respect."

"It's never a flaw to feel for others, Your Grace. Even if we should be privileged with more than some people, it's every person's duty to humanity to have sympathy for the less fortunate."

In silence they rode the short jaunt to the cliffs. The snow, crisp and clean, deepened off the road and they slowed to tread carefully. The ground literally vanished under the foot of whiteness and any step could be over a hazardous hole.

Katerina stopped her horse and dismounted. In her experience, men all thought women frail and helpless. Dax might appreciate a woman who didn't whine or wait to be catered to.

She held her reins out for a guard to take her gelding. "I like to think of this as the edge of the world." She led Dax to the rim of the cliff.

"Impressive as well as dangerous." He took her arm and pulled her back from the edge.

"I know and that's what makes it exciting." She sighed.

The water made a musical whoosh that captivated and hypnotized. It drew her back to the brim. The waves crashed against the rocks far below and she stood riveted by the magnificent sight.

A tremor shook the ground. It brought an instant alarm. The snow-covered earth shifted out from under her feet and she felt herself move slowly down until Dax jerked her back safely against him.

Locked in his arms, she avoided his reprimanding gaze.

"You should have heeded my warning."

"You couldn't have known we'd have an earthquake."

She looked back, watching part of the cliff slip away. It plummeted to the rocky sea below. She could have been a part of the seascape and yet, looking into Dax's eyes, she found a safe calmness knowing he'd not let that happen.

"I always anticipate the worst of conditions." He held her tight.

Katerina appreciated the worry in his eyes.

The earth shook again and she trembled. Dax squeezed her closer. The heat of him enveloped her in a dreamy fantasy. She leaned, seeking his kiss.

"As I said, dangerous." His abrupt release surprised her.

Katerina stepped away feeling she had been rescued and mocked at the same time. She tugged her hood snug to her head and placed her muffler up to her nose as the cold nipped at her skin.

"Accidents do happen," she retorted, unwilling to accept his chastising tone.

"Are you warm enough, Your Highness?"

"Have you a suggestion?"

Boldly forward, hopeful for the excitement he managed to create, she watched for signs he might choose to take her back into the circle of his arms. The thought lingered heatedly in her veins.

"I don't mean like going back to the palace until summer either," she added.

Determined to test the waters, she moved toward him. Balthazar told her to let the duke know her feelings. She couldn't simply blurt out, *I think I'm falling in love with you*, but she could express it in little ways.

"I haven't a suitable suggestion." He pulled a scarlet wool scarf from around his neck. "Do you have earth tremors like this often in Alluvia?"

"Sometimes it seems they never stop." She pointed to the far-off mountain. "It's that volcano."

He nodded. "That would be a warm place." He lifted his arms over her head with the scarf. "If we'd gone there we wouldn't have frost on our noses." He brushed a finger over hers.

If she hadn't been numb, she might have felt the touch.

"My brother has a very misguided sense of adventure. I love this place. However, its breathtaking beauty is better on warmer days."

He laughed. "My sister doesn't mind." He tied the scarf so it held her hood together, framing her face.

She swallowed when his hand wrapped the end of the scarf. No one would suspect his mindless action had meaning to her.

"This morning, I shouldn't have—" His face came closer to hers.

Katerina didn't want to hear he'd made a mistake. Guilt for giving her pleasure could only be a new level of rejection. She pressed her cold lips to his, deeply afraid it would be the last time she'd ever have the chance.

"Princess, don't." He pulled away.

Her heart shattered. She wanted to run, but his grip on her arm prevented her from leaving.

"Princess, wait. I didn't mean it as you think."

She looked up.

"Nothing would please me more than to continue where we left off this morning, except your brother approaches with my sister." His hand slid down and clasped her gloved fingers. "It's not appropriate for me to devour you in a kiss with your brother as a witness to my lust. I fear he'd have his guards shoot me for the misdeed."

She liked the plausible excuse. His expression softened and she accepted the sincerity because she wanted to trust him.

The creases at the corners of his eyes were a new delight for her to examine. She lifted her hand to his face, hoping to tell him Balthazar had no objections to their involvement. Before she actually touched the fan of lines, his other hand caught hers midair and pulled it down.

"Soon, Princess, very soon I'll provide you with everything you want."

An amazing thrill raced through Katerina. Her heart thumped with anticipation. Dax couldn't know how eager she was to hold onto the promise of intimacy. She had trouble believing how different her life seemed since he'd come along.

Dax let go of her hands and turned to the shouts of Balthazar.

"Is it not as magnificent as any shores you've seen, Maltar?" Balthazar helped Giselle from her horse and, even as they approached, he kept her hand locked in his.

Katerina loved the way her brother exuded happiness when enthralled by something. Giselle had him acting like the young boy Katerina recalled from their childhood.

She looked at the duke, wanting the same. Only the duke had released his hold on her hand.

"Amazing, Your Highness. Very much worth the trip, as are all the intimate splendors of your kingdom."

"Oh, what others have you seen?" Katerina asked, not believing he meant her.

He turned and Katerina lowered her lashes. He teased her with his lustful gaze. Had he no shame in the way he played with her heart?

Chapter Twenty

Dax lifted a brow when Katerina's gaze met his. Her desire matched his and he inched closer. Lifting a hand to take hers, their gloved fingers bumped, and then the blasting pop of a musket ceased the slow gravitational-like pull between them.

He claimed the princess with a swift grasp of her wrist and yanked her into the shelter of his body. Looking at Giselle, his gaze followed his sister's movements to the ground. The yelp he heard came from the prince.

"Balthazar!" Giselle knelt alongside the prince, plucked a glove from her fingers and placed it over the laceration on his cheek.

Dax looked in all directions for the gunman. He held the stunned princess, preventing her from leaving him.

"I have to go to him," Katerina insisted.

He led her to her brother and left her.

"You two look that way and you others spread out over there." He pointed with a sweep of his arm, ordering the guards. No one hesitated to obey. No one questioned his authority.

"Your Highness, I would suggest you stay down behind this rock with Giselle. It will give the two of you cover from an assassin's second attempt. I'll keep the princess safe with me."

"I don't want to go," Katerina argued.

"You haven't a choice." Dax grabbed her arm, towing her away from her brother.

"You should have let me stay with Balthazar." She shook free of his hand.

"The place was only big enough to safely accommodate two. Now stay down, Your Highness." He put her behind another boulder. "Giselle will look after the prince."

"Where are you going?" her voice squeaked as he rose.

He so loved to look at her, the smooth complexion of her face and the gentle sweep of her nose attaching to her cheek. The curve to her jaw reminded him of all the places on her he hadn't kissed.

"To find out how, with a detail of guards, someone managed to shoot at the prince." He stooped down, took her hand and held it to his face. "Stay back here until I return. Don't come out. Do you understand, Katerina?"

"Of course I—" She stopped and stared at him oddly.

"What's wrong?"

"You said my name."

"You can formally address my impertinence at a later time." Dax peered around the edge of rock.

"No." The word rushed out of her lips leaving them slightly parted, wholesomely inviting.

"Very well, don't accept my apology. I still want you to hide behind this rock. Do I make myself clear?"

"No." She grabbed his sleeve, preventing him from getting up. "I mean yes, I'm not an imbecile. It's the other I said no to. I like the way you say my name."

Could anything warm his icy limbs more? He thought not. The admission sealed their fates—he wanted her for more than a plan.

"Aren't you going to say anything?"

"Like what? You've left me speechless."

Her eyes twinkled with a bright happiness she rarely displayed. He leaned forward and kissed her. She held her gloved hand against his cheek and he fought the urge to drag her up from the ground and into his arms.

"I want you safe, Katerina. Now let go so I can be sure the coast is clear to get you and the prince away to a safer location."

"Wait." She looked truly worried for him. "What are you going to do? You haven't a musket."

"I still have to go. I suspect the assassin might have been one of the guards."

"You think a guard shot Balthazar?"

"I saw only seven of your guardsmen when we know there should be eight. I want to ask each of them about the others. They might have noticed the disappearance."

"Well if he's gone, what difference would it make? Please, Dax."

"Princess, stay here and I'll be right back. I have no other options."

Dax peered around the rock and before he took his first step, she grabbed his coat. He didn't like the frightened expression marring her features with worry lines. He hated how strong she thought she had to be as a woman and a ruler. Call him chauvinistic, but he appreciated she allowed him to know she needed to be taken care of. He had to admit, he had learned a great deal in their limited conversations.

"What is it?" He glanced at her, then the surroundings.

The guards were all over the place searching the rocky terrain, hunting behind the scattering of snow-dusted boulders.

He counted eight men and wondered if he'd counted wrong before.

"Please be careful."

"I always am, Princess." He pushed his hood from his head and smiled. "I'll be back for you shortly."

She stayed hunched down for only as long as it took him to move out from behind the rock. He gave her an angry glare and she ducked out of his line of sight.

Dax hoped whoever had tried to assassinate Prince Balthazar saw it was fruitless to try again. He had not studied the faces of the guards when they left the palace. Looking over them now, he recognized three. Lax in his observance, he'd let eight men trail them to the cliffs without considering one of them a danger.

Katerina was to blame. Even bundled up like a woolly polar bear, her intoxicating beauty distracted him. His concentration slipped from his predetermined mission.

"I wish to inspect everyone's musket," he commanded.

The guards approached. Did any of them take notice what the others did? He took each weapon and held it to his nose. The scent of gun smoke lingered in the air, yet none of the guns the men carried had been used to shoot the prince.

He looked over the guards again. Which of them had it been? Not one trembled with the fear of being found out. No one failed to stare him in the eye.

"Damn," he swore under his breath. Not one of them looked guilty, yet he was sure.

When they had broken into two groups at the palace, it seemed more likely the assassin had been with him and the princess. If not, the traitor might have gotten the job taken care of before Balthazar and Giselle reached the cliffs. Though that too would have put the man in a precarious position of getting caught by the other three guards.

Dax went over the other facts disturbing him. Why did the assassin wait until they were away from the palace? Too many ifs and not enough answers. It certainly had to be a guard among them. But which man left the group, shot a musket and disposed of it? If there was another musket, he could be sure it was tossed over the cliff. The heavy snow slowed everyone's movements.

The threat lurked amidst them. The probability of possible conspirators at the castle made it necessary to move forward with his altered plans for the prince and princess.

Hurrying through the snow, Dax stooped down behind the boulder with the prince and Giselle.

"Your Highness, I suspect it is one of the guards who shot you. If you would trust my judgment, I'd like you to go to a safe place with my sister."

"Back to the palace?" Balthazar stood up.

"No, somewhere that Giselle and I know will be much safer. The palace would not be a good idea. There could be other assassins there as well, ready to do the deed if you should return."

"Yes, I understand what you mean."

Dax hugged Giselle, whispering instructions in her ear. "Take him to the ship and let no one know who he is along the way. Make up whatever story you need to, but don't tell the prince the truth."

Giselle nodded, misty-eyed and afraid—for him and for the prince, Dax suspected.

"My sister?" Balthazar asked.

"I will safeguard her, Your Highness. I think it wise that you travel separately and go ahead with Giselle. But no guards, we can't trust them. I'll send them back to the palace and then bring the princess in a day to the safe place my sister knows to take you."

"You do a great service in assisting us, Maltar. I consider you a friend to the crown and to me personally." Balthazar took Giselle to her horse.

Dax kept his gaze on the guards while the prince and Giselle left. He returned to Katerina. She met him with her arm raised, rock in hand.

"I see that you at least don't sit idly by, waiting for everyone to protect you."

"What is going on?" She dropped the rock in the snow.

"Someone wants the prince dead, quite possibly the both of you." He grabbed her arm and pulled her to stand.

"I assumed that much."

From the tone of her voice, Katerina's anger masked her fear.

"What realms have you conquered lately?"

"I resent the implication we are pillagers and barbarians of neighboring nations. We have no enemies and have not seized lands from anyone in over a hundred years. My grandmother and my father each ruled with a firm hand. They were loving people and saw no reason to dominate other kingdoms."

She tugged on her arm. At first, he didn't want to let her go. He wanted to hold her and explain everything away as if it were all a bad dream.

"He's gone," Dax said as he released her.

Katerina ran to where the prince no longer hid.

"Where's Balthazar?" she cried. "Where are my guards?"

Her hands lifted to her head and he guessed a headache drew her fingers to her temples.

"Under my advisement, he's gone with Giselle. I ordered the guards to return to the palace." After removing his gloves, he touched her temples.

"Stop that." She swatted.

"Relax."

"He wouldn't leave me here. Not with you." She looked at the tracks in the snow. "Balthazar would never leave if I were in danger."

"Come, Princess, it's cold."

She jerked free, pushing her hands against his chest in frustration.

"He couldn't have just left me." Teary-eyed, she surveyed the area in disbelief.

"You're both in danger. Now come with me." He dragged her to her horse. "I promised the prince I would see to your safety."

Chapter Twenty-one

The stumbling walk to her horse was short. Katerina mounted with the duke's help and she looked at the trail ahead for signs of her brother waiting, or his return when he came to his senses.

"It's your sister." She fumed. "He's got his head in the clouds because of the spell she's put on him."

"Then he's not the only one bound by some woman's enchantment."

She shot a quick glance his way. With his angry tone, he couldn't have given her another compliment.

Snow flurries floated around Katerina's face. If the day had been normal, she would have caught the flakes on her tongue and savored the icy freshness. The trail Dax used took them the long way to the palace and, while she was familiar with it, she wondered how the duke knew the winding route.

They traveled slowly through deep clean snow. When they came to a road used by locals, the snow turned into the mud. The mixture of dirt and melting ice formed a quagmire of filth that splattered up the horse's legs. Katerina stopped at the fork in the path. She looked up at the palace on the hill and the road snaking invisibly beneath the snow.

"That's not the way," she called to him, pointing in the right direction.

"It's the route we take."

"I'll not go anywhere with you on your say so."

She turned her horse's head and snapped her riding crop against his rump. Traveling up the hill, around the curves and into the turn of the road, Katerina made a frenzied dash to her secure haven, her home.

She heard the harrumph of the duke's horse coming close behind. The drifts of snow hindered her speed and she jumped from her mount the moment Dax's hand snatched her reins. She fell to her knees. Her coat flew open and the cold wetness soaked through her gown.

"Katerina, you can't go back."

She managed to get to her feet to run.

"Princess, I'm trying to help." Dax grabbed her.

His strength enveloped her waist. He gave her no room to struggle as he tackled her and they fell into the snow. She had no recourse with his weight atop her.

"You're abducting me like some thief."

"Nonsense."

"It's not. You wormed your way into the palace, distracted my brother and me until you could find the opportunity to kill us."

"Really, and you don't think I might have done that sooner?"

"No...yes...I don't know." She didn't like how much he confused her.

"I'm not who you must fear. I promise I'm taking you someplace safe."

"I demand you take me to the castle."

"Sorry, but that's not possible." He got to his feet and hauled her up.

"You can't force me to go anywhere."

"Actually, I can." He lifted her up and flung her over his shoulder.

"Put me down you big ox. How dare you manhandle me in such a fashion," she shrieked, pounding on his back.

The scarf came undone and floated to the ground. She reached to grab it and missed.

"Wait," she pleaded.

She had the absurd need to keep the scarf as if it offered her security.

Dax stopped. "What?"

"The scarf fell in the snow."

He turned around. "So it has."

"Well get it back."

He laughed, but he walked over and snatched it up. It might have seemed silly to him, her having a sentimental attachment to the strip of knitted wool, but she did.

"Now put me down." Katerina kicked out of frustration.

"Princess, you're drawing the eyes of people who may have no choice but to tell an assassin which way you're headed." He dropped her on her feet.

Her hood fell back and the cold whipped around her head. The suddenness pained her temples and the place just behind her eyes. The tears she'd suppressed flowed in warm streams over her icy cheeks. She grasped her head, unable to deal with the shooting, the duke and a headache.

Dax tugged her hood back in place. One hand slid to the back of her head and the other arm circled her body.

"Will you please cooperate and get on my horse?" He held her to him and she didn't resist the comfort.

She didn't want to say yes or no. Usually everything she did was on her terms and not those dictated to her. The palace sat atop the hill and appeared close, yet she knew it had to be a mile away.

"Is my brother all right?" She hid her sob behind a cough.

"The last time I saw him, he and Giselle were on horses. I had them head out before I let the guards go."

He stroked a soothing hand up and down her back. She liked it, but didn't let go of her distrust of him.

"We need to leave now. People are watching."

Katerina looked at the closest house—windowpanes were filled with interested faces.

Katerina nodded, letting her cheek brush against the front of his coat. She picked up a hint of his soap-clean scent. It drew her nose up and her gaze went immediately to his. The duke's breath touched her face. He'd eaten something fruity. She hadn't eaten breakfast at all, figuring she'd do so after what was to be a short outing. The scent of spiced apple made her hungry. His mouth moved closer, making her thirsty for one taste of him.

"Let's get you in the saddle." His head turned sharply. "I'm afraid your horse has gone on his own journey, so we'll have to ride together."

His hand went firmly to her back and they walked to his horse.

"Where are we going if not to the palace?"

"A friend's house." He interlaced his fingers and held the newly formed foothold down for her to step in.

She put her muddied boot in the sling of his joined hands and he boosted her onto the saddle. Immediately, before she had a chance to adjust, Dax swung up behind her. Katerina stiffened in surprise when his arm strongly cinched her back to his bulkiness.

"Whose house are we going to? I look a dreadful mess to walk into anyone's home."

"It's just a friend and no one you would know."

"Not know? How absurd," she scoffed. "I know all nobles to some extent. Maybe not each single individual, but their family names are all known. Is it some woman with whom you stay?"

"Yes."

She cringed inside at his chuckle.

"And you will not tell me who she is so I might prepare myself?"

She surveyed her surroundings wondering if she might plot an escape. She had no wish to meet anybody while looking as if she just crawled out of a pigsty. Nor could she face someone he may have been intimate with before coming to her palace.

"Prepare how?"

"Mentally."

"Un-huh, and you do this for what reason?"

"Well obviously she's going to be impressed to have me in her home. I'll have to accept apologies for her untidy house even if it's clean enough to eat off the floor and then I'll have to listen to boring gossip she'll feel compelled to tell me."

"Not everyone feels a gripping need to repeat rumors."

"Besides that, my headache lingers and if I don't remind myself how necessary you think this is, then I'll be a horrible houseguest. Therefore, I'll need to concentrate on being pleasant."

"So much work." His tone had a light marveling ring.

"It is work and if you had to rule a country you'd know what I'm talking about. Everyone expects me or Balthazar to know how to solve any problem and while I can most times, I worry I might say something wrong and offend someone."

"Did you ever consider relaxing with the idea, no one requires you to be perfect?"

"My father was."

"I doubt that."

"You didn't know him. He always said or did the right thing. The people of Alluvia loved him and...and I think they hate me."

"No one hates you."

"Ha! You don't know me."

Dax's hand rubbed over her coat in a comforting gesture. He'd not know how the movement stirred her insides. Her nipples puckered from the stimulation much quicker than from the cold.

"This woman you know, is she not from here?"

"She's lived in Alluvia all her life as far as I'm aware."

"Then why wouldn't she know who I am? Every noble in the kingdom has attended one function or another at the palace. I'm a prominent figure and she would have seen me even if we've not been introduced."

"Don't stress too much, my princess. She'll not likely recognize you."

"I think you're wrong."

"She's not a noblewoman, Your Highness. I highly doubt she's ever seen you."

“You’re staying with peasants, commoners, but why on heaven would you do that?” She wished she could see his face. “For those traveling a great distance to attend, our invitations to the ball offered residency at the homes of nobles.”

“I wasn’t invited.”

Katerina felt as if she sucked in a fly or a beetle. She shook away the idea the duke had anything to do with the incident that morning. Her sudden coughing attack led the duke to rub at her back.

“Are you all right?”

“No. The plot thickens and I don’t know how you fit in it. Balthazar is shot and gone. You’re kidnapping me. What’s next? To tell me you aren’t even a duke?”

He cleared his throat and she froze.

“You’re not, are you? What term do I use for you, sir?”

“We’ll talk of this later.”

She sat quiet for a minute. It sunk deeper into her mind that she was in trouble.

“Where are we really going?”

“Somewhere out of open range.”

“I wouldn’t have been exposed to danger in my palace.”

“I don’t know that.”

“I want to see Balthazar.”

“The prince is being looked after and I’m afraid I can’t let the two of you be together.”

“Why?”

“When we get to a warm place, I’ll explain.” He nuzzled her face alongside her hood. “I’ll not let any harm come to you, my princess.”

His affectionate tone perplexed her. She sat quiet, cold and dreadfully worried about Balthazar. Apparently Dax sensed her anxiety and gave her a gentle squeeze.

The villages they passed through were small, poorly-created clusters of buildings with muddy roads that spilled onto doorsteps. A couple of miles and three villages later, Dax stopped at a bungalow with a spiraling column of thick black smoke. Sparks, like the kind only pinecones and sap created, spit from the top of a crooked chimney. Quaintly lopsided, the house had a window on each side of the door and it appeared the dwelling grinned.

Dax dismounted first and held his arms up to her.

"This is the house?" She swung a leg over, put her hands on his shoulders and slipped into his arms.

"Yes."

She felt feminine, womanly and strangely happy. His towering height excited her, but there was more she enjoyed in his presence.

"Does this woman mean something to you?" She continued with her self-torturous prying into his personal life.

"Like how?"

She shrugged, not knowing how to ask intimate questions.

Dax smiled as if he knew exactly what she asked. She had a sudden thought that this woman might be the reason he didn't want to court her. Except there were other facts to consider, like he was not a duke and had not been invited to her ball.

"Is she in on the plan to abduct me?"

"No and it would be wise if you were not to speak of such things around her." He took her elbow and led her closer to the house.

"Why? Doesn't she know what you're doing?"

"Princess—" He twisted her to face him.

"Yes?" If anyone should display impatience it should be her.

"Princess, you're not in any danger from me."

"So you say."

Chapter Twenty-two

Dax couldn't help himself around the lovely princess. He didn't like to distress her. It wrinkled her face and put a horrid darkness in her charming velvet brown eyes. He preferred her less vulnerable.

While Katerina stared at the modest hovel, he saw a trace of a smile. The stone walls were low and the roof sagged with the weight of snow. It would not be anything to which she was used to and still, she looked past him with a hint of an adventurous spirit.

The door of the house opened.

"Your Highness." The old woman came bustling out wrapped in a heavy sheepskin cloak.

"See, she knows me," Katerina huffed with an indignant tone.

"Wait here." He contained his laugh.

Walking to the woman, hooded and shadowed beneath the dingy fur wrap, he put an arm around her and moved her away from the princess.

"Are you here alone?" He spoke low.

"Why yes. I kept it warm, just as you wanted. But beggin' your pardon, I thought you and the other lady would be back last night."

"We had a change of plans." He took a breath, thinking how much everything continued changing from moment to moment.

The woman looked curiously at Katerina. The possibility of her knowing the princess was slim, but still chancy. He found it best if he kept the two of them apart.

"Wait one moment," he told the woman, and went to Katerina.

"And here I thought the woman you were staying with might be some—"

He raised a brow, hoping she'd say what was on her mind instead of bottling it up.

"Oh, never mind."

He made no comment, for he had none. All the while he let her believe and worry about going to a noble's house he discovered it disturbed her more to think she'd be facing his mistress.

He put his hands on her shoulders and turned her toward the open doorway. "Go inside and get warm. I've arrangements to make with this woman and then I'll join you."

"What arrangements?"

"You'll know when the time is right." He put a hand on her back and pushed her over the threshold.

"But..."

"Stay inside." He pulled the door shut and went back to the old woman.

"Do you have another place to spend the night while I borrow your house again?" he asked the woman. "I know our arrangement was for only two nights."

"No, no, not to worry. My brother lives over that way." She pointed. "You're welcome for as long as you need. Be sure when you return to your home, to tell my son he can return."

"I'll reward your son well for having a generous mother. If I can talk him into coming home to you, I will."

"My son is a stubborn one. Many years ago, when he worked in the palace, something happened he would not tell me about. He only said it was necessary for him to go away."

"He was young. Maybe he just thought an adventurous life would be worth pursuing."

Her head bobbed and she looked up to him. "Maybe I could serve you something to eat before I go."

She peered around him in an attempt to figure out why he returned with a different woman. The day before, he rented her home for him and his sister. With the arrival of a different young lady, he could well imagine her thoughts.

"We can manage." He took out money and put it in her hand. "Take this for your trouble."

"Oh no, you have paid me well."

"And that was for two nights. This is for my final night, for tomorrow I head for Volda."

Dax watched the woman waddle across the road to another house. She disappeared inside and he turned to enter his residency for the night. He drew his shoulders back and braced himself to face Katerina and her questions.

Within the warm, one-room dwelling, he found the princess standing in front of the fire, rubbing her gloved hands together. She paced a few steps one way and a few back.

"So, why am I here and just who are you?"

Leaving her to speculate would not help him figure her out. Neither would bluntness. Each minute he remained on the Isle of Alluvia, he and Giselle were dangerously close to losing everything they loved. Fighting for his home seemed easy enough before immersing himself in Katerina's life. Whatever he said would hurt her pride.

Katerina's serious determination added fire to her eyes.

"Do you think we could warm up before the war?"

The morning's events had kicked all of his plans out of sync.

"What war? Who's going to war? I told you we don't—"

"It's a figure of speech, Princess." He chuckled.

He understood her complete confusion. In some ways, it seemed a blissful state not to know what could be going on.

"Who is she?"

Dax looked at the closed door and thought of the woman and her tired face. Wrinkles hung like aged leather. Eyes, deep into the sockets, had long suffered sadness of not knowing where her son had gone.

"No one in particular."

He watched Katerina drop her gloves on the old worn table. She strolled back to the fireplace, advancing like a moth to a flame. With her palms out, she wiggled her fingers in front of the heat.

"She *is* someone. Just how you know her is what I find interesting. There are closer villages to my palace and the same kind and generous Alluvian peasants for you to have paid for their home. Why this place, so far from where you were going?"

"I know her son." He reluctantly gave in to answering some of her unimportant questions.

"How? You're not from here." She turned her head slightly. "You're not from Maltar either, I imagine?"

"Enough questions." He tossed his coat over the back of a chair and slipped Katerina's from her arms. "Are you cold?"

"My feet feel like ice, like they could snap off."

She sat on the chair near the fire and rubbed her hands together to stimulate circulation. Dax knelt and picked up her foot. She surprised him by not asking anything more about who he was.

"What are you doing?" Her fingers curled around the seat of the chair.

"Kneeling before royalty."

"As you should," she sputtered, when he clamped his fingers around the back of her calf.

"Does a man on his knees arouse all your senses, or just me?"

"You arouse nothing in me." Her sharp intake of air rose up her chest and made him anticipate her every word.

Dax untied her wet, sleek, sealskin boots and slipped them off. No stockings or socks covered her petite feet.

"Now what are you doing?"

"Helping you get warm."

"I can do it—myself," her voice whispered with a catch.

"Not as well as I can."

The banter stimulated erotic desires he'd not been aware of until her. If she had fantasies, he didn't want to disappoint her.

He held fast to her leg as she tried to take her foot away. With her heel cupped in his cold palm, he massaged the slim dainty foot with solid swift strokes. Her cold toes wiggled each time his fingers glided along the bottom and lingered on the smooth arch.

"Ticklish, Princess?" He put her foot down and lifted the other.

"No."

He slid his hand along the sole with a feather-light touch.

"Stop that." Her mouth pinched tight in an obvious attempt not to smile or laugh.

"I'll ask again, are you ticklish, Katerina?"

A burble of a laugher started and then more.

"All right, yes."

"How ticklish, Katerina?" He bent his head and breathed a puff of hot air along her ankle.

A sultry purr followed the pause in her breathing. He continued caressing her foot as if it were the only part of her he had a right to make love to.

He dragged his lips across her toes, beneath to her sole and back up the other side. She sat mute with a porcelain doll smile frozen on her face. The immobile gaze of her eyes hypnotized him. Her trance persisted and he took advantage of her silent acceptance. He moved over her foot, giving each elegant toe his full attention. The coldness of her skin prevented them from sweating, so they smelled as clean as she had the night before. Her perfumed soaps, scented waters and fragranced oils heightened the awareness of his senses.

"You're delicious, Princess."

He licked the top of her foot. Kissing a straight line with sensuous touches to her skin, he moved along her shinbone and stopped at her knee. Not because he didn't want to go further.

Dax had every intention of finding the center of her soul.

"It seems the way is blocked." He lifted his head. "Katerina?"

"Don't try using my name like some love spell. I'm past that dreadfully embarrassing moment when I told you I liked the way you say it."

She pushed her hands tighter over her dress against her thighs to prevent him from going higher. He tested her resistance only once, then stood.

He turned to inspect the stew simmering in an iron pot over the fire. "Hungry?"

"How can you think of food now?"

He glanced back at her.

"You know you're impossible."

"I know, Princess. You make it hard for a man to resist." He spooned out a bowl of the delicious smelling lamb stew. "Here, eat something. It'll help warm your insides."

He shucked off his jacket and pulled at the knotted cravat no longer neatly tied at his throat.

"I'm not hungry."

"You've not eaten all day."

"Only because you insisted on riding all day, to bring me here for a reason you have yet to divulge."

"I wanted to get you far from the threat of harm."

"And yet I'm in the middle of danger every minute I spend with you."

"You're not in peril with me, Princess. I mean you, nor your brother, any harm."

"I hope you don't mind if I don't trust your word."

"That is your prerogative."

Dax sat opposite her at the table. She kept her back to him and it allowed him a long inspection of her. She would be such a treat to kiss all over again.

Chapter Twenty-three

The room hardly had the space to allow her privacy, let alone a good long walk. She couldn't stand him watching her because she wanted everything she saw in his eyes and felt in his touch. She retreated from the idea he would resume his seduction.

Returning to their earlier conversation, she pressed to know at least one true thing about him.

"What's your real name?"

She watched the well-defined muscles beneath Dax's shirt. It was hard not to notice and recall the strength of his hold.

"Daxton."

"That's it? No title?"

"Daxton James Kent the fourth if the long version is what you wish to know."

"It shows your family's longevity if you're the fourth to bear the name. It's something, I suppose." She put a spoonful of the stew in her mouth and chewed a piece of meat.

Dax kicked the remaining empty chair out from under the table. A clumsy man would have knocked the rickety thing over with the swift move. Lifting his long legs encased in wool trousers, he propped his feet on the seat, ankles crossed. Tilting back his chair on two legs, he stretched, showing off a slew of new ripples. Katerina found the impertinence less insulting since she had grown fond of watching of him. He locked his fingers together behind his head while he studied her and no doubt devised a new lie. She wanted answers and she wanted truthful ones. His relaxed pose produced more lines of muscle. From legs to crotch, her gaze followed the contours with curiosity.

"Will you tell me now what's going on?" she finally asked.

"I don't know, Princess. I still think a guard took the shot at the prince. I checked each man's musket for the lingering scent of discharge and none of them were used. It doesn't mean they didn't have another they tossed into the sea."

"You expect me to believe you had nothing to do with the events today."

"I'm not behind the plot to assassinate you or your brother." His fingers drummed the table softly. "If I were, you would not be here."

Katerina clung to that answer as a lifesaver. He could have easily killed her in the throne room, her bedchambers or let her slide over the cliff. Balthazar's death could have been just as uncomplicated.

She turned her gaze from his and looked at the fire.

"How long will we stay here?"

"Just the night."

"And then you'll take me home?"

"Yes."

"Good. You'll see then how wrong it was for you to keep me from the palace. There are guardsmen and lords who need to be informed of the attempt on my brother's life."

"We'll be going to *my* home, Katerina."

"Yours?" Her gaze swung back to his.

"I can't let you go back to the palace. One assassin or several may be waiting for you."

"I simply cannot believe any of our guards would want my brother dead. They've been very loyal and trustworthy." She pushed the bowl away, too upset to eat.

"Princess, this will not be the last attempt."

"How long do you plan on keeping me there, at your home? I can't just abandon mine on the chance someone might try to kill me."

She rose from the chair with a need to escape the small room. The fear she was letting Dax get away with too much agitated her. That she wasn't frightened of him left her further befuddled.

Her strides to the door weren't quick, but they were direct.

"You can't go home." Dax rushed from the chair when she touched the latch to get free.

"You can't boss me around." She twisted to confront him head on.

"You haven't even got on your boots or your coat. You'd freeze to death."

Katerina wanted to cry. His presence stripped her of power and left her weak.

"Please." She leaned her forehead against him. "I just want to go home."

"In due time, Princess." He pulled her closer and she willingly took comfort from his embrace. He made her forget bad things.

"You said you weren't invited to my ball." She didn't know if she wanted details. "You said you didn't want to court me. Was it Giselle you hoped to marry off to my brother?"

"It didn't start anything like you're thinking. I actually forbade Giselle to fall in love with the prince. As for me, I did come to see you. However, while I said I wasn't there to court you, my statement became a lie from that point onward."

Katerina lifted her head and looked at him. His words brightened the dull spot in her soul.

"I met you. I talked to you. And I've tasted you." He stroked the side of her face. "You've changed my mind about many things I had planned and thought. I can assure you, I have no intention of courting you."

She pushed to be free of him. He built up her hope and crushed it with his statement.

"Hold on there, Princess." He tugged her back. "Katerina, I have no intention of courting you or following some protocol where you play hard to get and I trail you like a puppy."

"Let me go." She struggled.

"Never." He gripped her chin and held it up to look into her eyes.

She stared back in confusion. He didn't want her, yet he wouldn't let go.

"Katerina, my beautiful princess, from the moment I met you, my destiny changed. I said no courting, because I'm going to marry you without the preliminaries."

"Marry me?"

"You sound surprised. It's what you wanted, what you need, isn't it?"

She nodded when she should have shaken her head. She didn't want to marry anyone. She had already decided to let Balthazar be the one to rule.

Chapter Twenty-four

Dax pulled her from the door. He knew little of her situation with her uncle. Questioning her and getting the story from the beginning seemed the best route to enlightenment.

"Tell me why you must marry soon and why someone would wish to kill the prince."

Her pretty lips pursed and she stared up at him as if she'd not say.

"What gives you the idea me or my brother have to marry soon?"

"Could be because a little birdie told me or it could be I guessed. You do mention marriage a lot, either for your brother or yourself."

"No, I don't," she said to be stubborn.

"You do. Now what is the deal?"

"You'll tell me why you're here?"

"I always planned to."

"It was my father's doing."

Dax gently guided her to the chair.

"What did he do?"

"He died." Her chest heaved with a heavy sigh. "Instead of naming an heir to the crown, he made Balthazar and me vie for the position. He wouldn't select one of us to succeed him. So whoever marries first, before the end of the month, gets to be ruler. Sounds like an awful child's game, but that's how it works."

She confirmed everything he already knew. So, it wasn't a bizarre tale Talbot had told him.

"And if neither of you should marry?"

"My uncle, Lord Talbot, is crowned king as the next in the royal line." Her fingers drummed on the table nervously. "He's an evil man who thinks he should rule everything. He's not satisfied with his small kingdom on the Isle of Elbian. I've heard rumors of his growing army and the threats he places on other kingdoms."

"What do you do? Offer to help?"

"How? When? To who?" She picked at a loaf of bread and ate little bites. "My father dealt with all this and if asked, he helped. We can't just go butting into someone else's business based on hearsay."

"Ah, like the lords and the grievances of their domestics."

"No, yes, something like that, but it's different."

"But you'd help?" He walked around and rubbed his jaw in the vee of his hand. He needed to shave, but it would have to wait until he got to the ship.

"Of course we would. If it were up to me, I'd have imprisoned my uncle, except he's not openly done anything wrong."

"What do you say to making a little trip, Princess?"

"Now? Where?"

"Volda."

"Volda? That's just a little island. What could be there to help me find out who the assassin is or who he was hired by?" She looked questioningly at him.

"Have you ever been to Volda, Princess? It's mountainous and has views similar to your cliffs, but it also has areas that roll down onto sandy shores. In the summer Volda is a nice ride on horseback and has the most amazing sight at night. The Northern Lights set the sky ablaze in a rainbow of colors. Purples and greens dance on the white sands and we can dance with them."

"You're being silly."

"Don't you like having fun sometimes?" He picked up her hand and kissed her knuckles.

"How is it you have such knowledgeable insight about a tiny little nothing of a place? It's so far north that it's really no good to anyone."

Dax let go and walked around the table. He picked up a chair a few inches from the floor and slammed it down. The sharp thud had its own repressed anger as he picked up the bowls from the table and put them in a wood dry sink.

"I spent time there," he snapped.

"When will we leave?"

"First light."

"We're going to sleep here?"

His momentary upset by her dismissal of his country fell by the wayside when she turned and examined the room. The place contained a narrow bed and very little other furniture. Dax grinned at her wide-eyed stare. She knew what he planned because he made no secret of how he wanted to make love to her.

"It's warm and the bed fits two." He sat on the edge and laughed at the shocked expression so beautifully covering her face with a salmon pink blush. "I was only joking, Your Highness. You can sleep on the bed. I'll make myself a spot on the floor."

"No, you're right. The bed does fit two."

She sat next to him. As bold as a whore, she put a hand on his thigh and bounced on the straw-stuffed mattress.

"Could be softer," she noted.

Dax swallowed and got up to add wood to the fire. He ignored her perplexity and sat at the table. Leaning back on two legs of the chair again, this time he propped his booted feet on the corner of the table. His assessment of Katerina went on for ten minutes without a word or a squeak from her. Plans formed, altered, and he grinned believing the princess really might like what he now considered.

"So, do we just sit here the rest of the day looking at the walls?" she asked.

"Yes."

"I don't like to sit still." She got to her feet and paced the small room. "Can't you suggest something we could do?"

Dax lifted a brow. "I'm not sure you would find my suggestion appropriate."

"Why, is it equally boring?" She stared out the filthy window.

Dax let the chair drop back down on all four legs.

"Not boring at all." He walked up behind her.

She stiffened at his touch and he rubbed her shoulders gently.

"Well are you going to tell me or will it remain a secret?" She twisted around.

"You really don't know what I'm suggesting, do you?" He cupped the side of her face.

She blinked and backed into the wall.

He moved his touch from her reddening cheek to her hip.

"You don't mean to propose we—" Her gaze shot to the bed and then back to him.

"What else is there?" He licked his lips.

He saw no real reason not to bed the beauty. After all, he would marry the delightful creature. It was more than he did for other women he'd taken as mistresses.

"I'll just read something."

Dax put a hand up to catch her rosy porcelain face.

"Would you really mind if I kissed you?"

Her eyelashes fluttered and she remained motionless. He touched his lips to hers tentatively and sipped at her mouth like an aged wine he savored.

Katerina clutched his shoulders and the chain reaction led them to the bed. Their feet shuffled one way and then the other, moving them closer to their destination. He kissed around her face, under her jaw and returned to her mouth. In the cradle of his arms, he lowered Katerina to the bed. Never letting her mouth free from his, he knelt on the mattress and hovered over her.

"Dax..." She breathlessly gasped for air, pressing her palms to his chest.

He held her head in his hand and traced a line around her mouth with his finger.

"You're not going to seduce me, are you?" Her hopeful voice caught with the trail of his finger down her neck.

The pressure of his fingers swept over her collarbone and elicited spirals of vibrantly warm sounds from her throat.

"As a highborn, Princess, you should never question what you know is the truth. Rather reject and fight the advances or allow what it is you want without inquiry." He kissed under her jaw.

"Get off me." She pushed at him. "You can't treat me as if I were a harlot."

"I thought I was treating you like a sex-starved woman."

Katerina hit his arms, forcing him to relinquish his hold.

"You have no right to think I should even want to be intimate with any man other than my future husband."

"Had I not made it clear that will be me, sweet princess?"

"Never." She hit him harder.

"A feisty lady always protests too much when she charms her way to within inches of a sexual encounter. It makes me think you prefer a little restraint to appease your guilt for wanting pleasure."

He sat and pulled her over his lap sideways.

"What are you doing?"

"Ah, my Katerina, you need to be punished for teasing me with your kisses." His hand caressed her bottom.

"You wouldn't dare strike me." She squealed when his splayed fingers whacked her ass.

After each blow her squeals became whines of protest and delight. He managed to pull her dress up, touching her bare thigh as he spanked her. His hand on her bottom forced her down upon the solid bulge of his erection.

"When I make love to you, I want to hear your cries of rapture."

She rubbed her cunt against him as he abused her with nothing more than love taps. Each playful smack he gave to her bottom came with whimpered requests.

"It will be screams of disgust," she moaned as the down sweep of his hand sent her into his aching groin.

"I want you uninhibited during our coupling. Whatever you feel is proper, discard it."

"You're a vile man to...to...oh God, please," she begged when his hesitation left her ass suspended without contact with his pulsing cock. "Please don't...stop."

He turned her over on his legs and pulled her up to kiss her face. Her fingers latched onto his shoulders and squeezed tighter when he kissed and sucked at the lobe of her ear. Wiggling was involuntary. Anticipatory thrills had her clinging as if he'd get away and leave her yearning unfulfilled.

"Dax." She squeaked out his name when his hand moved over the garment and pushed at her breast.

With each passing minute, Dax drew her more and more into his deceptive game. He had her body panting to be sated by him. She took the paddling with the desire of a wanton. With each rasp of his name, she tugged at invisible threads attached to his aching soul. She allowed him to spank her and another dimension formed around their impending union.

Abruptly, he couldn't handle the way his emotions spun out of control. The woman in his arms obsessed him. Sliding her from his lap, he got up from the bed. He needed air and a chance to think.

"If we're to leave first thing in the morning, I should see about procuring a sleigh for our horse."

Dax made a swift departure from the bungalow. His plot with Giselle was to distract and alienate the prince and princess from prospective consorts, not fall in love. The inclusion of a killer into the scheme made his revised plans even more necessary than his feelings for Katerina did.

Across the way he had spotted a sleigh in front of a barn. He went there and found the owner.

"Good evening, sir." The man greeted him with a bow.

"I wish to purchase your conveyance and a horse." He looked at the sleigh and while it was small, it would be sufficient.

"Will this do? I have another—a better one in the barn."

"This will be adequate. I'll need it outfitted with lots of furs, food and water. I have a long way to travel and I don't wish my lady friend to suffer too much discomfort." He looked at the bungalow and saw Katerina's outline in the window.

"I'll be glad to see that everything is to your liking, sir. I'll also personally take care of having the rig ready for you when you wish it." He patted his hands, warming them together in the big mitts of wool.

"Early tomorrow morning."

"It will be ready, tonight."

Dax had snatched his coat up, but left his gloves behind and the pockets were hardly sufficient to keep his own hands warm. He withdrew the last of his money and handed it to the man.

"This is too generous, m'lord. The sleigh is old." The man's face was hardly visible. A scarf of blue-dyed woven wool covered the lower half so that only dark brown and curious eyes stared out.

"It serves my needs." Dax glanced up to see Katerina still at the window.

Chapter Twenty-five

A lone tear skittered down Katerina's face and she irritably swiped it away with the back of her hand. Dax was in for a startling enlightenment if he thought he could tease her with desire and then expect anything more from her than a cold welcome on his return to the hut. It didn't matter if inside she cried harder than imaginable. The brute was not going to get any satisfaction in seeing her weep over him.

Staring through the sooty glass of the window, she spotted him talking to someone a good distance away. While her thoughts drifted to Balthazar, she had to decide what to do for herself. Going along with Dax's mysterious plan would be foolish, especially since she didn't know what he wanted from her. Pacing the small room with its limiting space made her dizzy. She picked up a jug from the table to get a drink and took a sip of the strong crowberry wine. The sweet liquor tasted good and, as her thirst grew more demanding, she drank in gulps instead of sips. It didn't help the headache much, but it made her care less about it.

During her wait, she took intermittent peeks at Dax through the dingy window. When he saw her, he turned away and his imposing rejection drove her back to the jug.

Ten, fifteen minutes had passed before she watched him trudge back toward the bungalow. He gave an exaggerated shiver upon his entrance. At the fire, he rubbed his hands together to warm them.

"What were you doing out there?" she demanded. "What could you possibly have to talk to a peasant about for twenty minutes?"

"It was a simple conversation between men." He pulled his coat off and rubbed at his arms. "And how do you know I'm not a peasant, too?"

"You couldn't possibility be one of them. Your clothing—"

"Is from the palace."

"They weren't the night of the ball."

"True."

"Your manners…well some of them, at least, are refined."

"Everyone can be taught to some extent."

"Your dialect, then. It gives away you're not from here."

"That I am not."

"Are you a peasant?"

"I can respond to that with a simple no." He turned from her and tossed another log on the fire.

"Nothing is simple for you, so what did you discuss with that man outside? Is he one of your cohorts?"

"I discussed with the gentlemen what we'll need for the trip in the morning. I have arranged for him to supply a sleigh."

"Oh." Katerina had known he was going to see about a sleigh, but she hadn't thought of anything beyond how she went about doing things at the palace. Her life was led by stating an order and it was done without question.

"You should get some sleep." Dax sat on the chair and tugged his boots off. "We'll leave very early and it will be a long ride."

He removed his socks and draped them over the back of a chair to dry. She tried not looking at his feet, but there they were—ten nice toes. She recalled the moment when he kissed her toes. Could she do the same to him? She thought not. The idea seemed weird. Yet, she did like the texture of his skin, what little she'd touched. His hands were not overly smooth like hers, but they didn't show signs of hard labor. His lips were firm and soft and a thrill to have caressing her skin. Now she seriously pondered what it would be like to kiss him in similar places, including his well-formed feet.

Dax freed the loose cravat from his neck and tossed it on the table. He unbuttoned his shirt down to his navel. She had the new delight of inspecting his chest. Lightly sprinkled with hair, his torso appeared as solid as it had felt under her hand earlier.

Katerina lay down and tried staring elsewhere. She refused to wish for him to join her. Throwing herself in the path of his lips exhausted her. Fuming from his last retreat, she still had the lingering hope he would change his mind and return to kiss her.

"I said before, the bed is wide enough for two. You need not inconvenience us both by taking some of the covers to the floor." She slid to the far side of the mattress, near the wall and gave him her back to stare at as she closed her eyes and waited.

"As you wish, Princess. However, the fire needs tending awhile."

She rubbed her eyes and let her mind settle with her failure to seduce a man. Her eyelids grew heavy under the cumbersome weight of questions she still didn't have answered. One topped her list. Why were they were making a trip to the far-off kingdom of Volda? She answered the question for herself as she remembered he said he was taking her to his home.

Before crawling into bed with her, Dax allowed enough time to pass for Katerina to fall asleep. He first thought she might stay awake out of lingering distrust of him. Yet, what woman after submitting to a spanking would still hold a fear for her safety?

Easing over, he tried to make the least disturbance to her peaceful position in the bed. Intentionally waiting for her to fall asleep had been a good idea, yet now he wished her to wake. Their fencing of words was like foreplay. Most women he met were too ready to throw themselves at him. Katerina's facade of disinterest never quite became believable since she made such sad whimpers when he withdrew. She amazed him with her fortitude at hanging onto her dignity and expressing her desires at the same time.

Dax closed his eyes and drifted off to sleep while thinking about his strong attraction for Katerina. It went beyond her beauty. When she shifted and rolled over, he opened his eyes. He turned to his side and looked at the serene expression on her face. As if she were locked in a nice dream, she smiled. Her hum of pleasure touched his heart and he slipped a hand over her middle. He wanted to hold her and his wish was granted. She moved, made another sweet little moan and snaked an arm over him. Her whole body wiggled, squirmed and cuddled against him as if he were her bed pillow.

As Katerina entwined herself with him, his heart ached. Her beauty made a nice trophy. The fragrance of her body engaged his lustful desires. However, his physical needs weren't the only thing he yearned to satisfy.

He pulled her closer. His intentions lost the steadfast ideal of allowing her to retain her virginity until their wedding night. He wanted to make her truly his before another hour passed.

As he shifted, Katerina's fingers dropped from his waist to his erection. He covered her hand and rubbed it along his shaft. Her sudden resistance told him she had awakened.

"Have you any idea the power you hold over a man by holding his cock?" he whispered, nuzzling his face against her soft hair.

"No." Her fingers moved slightly.

"It is the real heart of the human male. It can be stroked until I fall victim to the delirium of a fool. You could probably ask me anything and I would answer merely based upon the grip of your slender fingers or the tenderness of your lips."

"M-my lips?"

"Yes." He touched her bottom lip and stuck his finger between her teeth. "Suck on it."

She surprised him and complied.

"Mmmm," he moaned letting his imagination run wild.

Her tongue swirled over the thrusts he made. Her teeth caught the tip before he pulled free. Her hand wrapped over his and she guided the moves, kissing not only his fingers, but his palm, his knuckles and his wrist.

His cock trembled in anticipation.

She sat up, sleepy faced and seductive. Her lashes fluttered to wash away her drowsiness and her hand rubbed his trousers steadily without his help. When her grip curved to examine the length and shape, he nearly lost control in his pants with her slow, methodical inspection.

Dax cupped her face. Her soft skin begged to be tasted. He reached to kiss her parted lips and she drew away from him.

"Katerina?" He questioned the mischievous glint in her eye.

Her fingers took a firmer hold, sliding her caress from the tip of his swollen cock to the base of the shaft. He wanted to retrieve the beast from his trousers and experience the silkiness of her petting touch. Instead, he remained still. As if she were a timid field mouse, he restrained himself from the slightest flinch.

She squirmed back, toward the foot of the bed.

"Come back here." He grabbed her arm.

"I'm not leaving," she whispered in her sleep-husky voice.

He let go because her gaze rolled downward. She saw what he did, his trousers tenting.

Katerina leaned toward his middle. She kissed his bare abdomen. Her fingers slipped up the center and lay over his pounding heart. She dragged her lips, a delicate trail downward. The pulse of his body and all his blood surged toward that one point.

"Oh God," he groaned when her mouth clamped over his cloth-covered cock.

She held still with her teeth firmly gripping the long hard shaft. He shuddered and fumbled to undress the devil she teased. He didn't want to know if she'd done this before. His mind wouldn't work with such complications to his emotions. His fingers didn't even cooperate. Thanks to Katerina, they didn't have to as hers replaced his and she easily opened his trousers.

Chapter Twenty-six

Katerina remembered the one and only time Stefan asked her to do this for him. She thought it strange and when she finished, she thought it a dirty secret they should never mention again. His idea of her drinking from him had insulted her. Especially when she watched his discharge hit the floor.

She opened Dax's trousers and worked his large cock into the open. Stefan could be called boy size. Dax had a thick, throbbing shaft of flesh long enough her fingers didn't reach from tip to base.

"I have power over you with this in my hand?"

He propped his head up on a folded pillow and looked at her with a dreamy expression. His half-closed eyes indicated he already experienced what Stefan told her was euphoria for a man.

"I said if you held your fingers in the right position," he answered.

"Oh?" Katerina rubbed under and over his magnificent cock. "I presume it's a secret I must discover myself. After all, you wouldn't want to divulge your plans by explaining how I should grip this, would you?"

The crowberry wine left her lightheaded and uninhibited. She didn't care. If felt wonderful to caress his arousal.

"You've my complete indulgent cooperation, Princess. I'll lie here and allow you time to figure out what hold might get you all you desire to know."

She squeezed the soft sac below the shaft. "And this?"

"Touch me gently there, Princess, if you wish to have children."

Katerina inhaled the comment with a measure of surprise. She grasped the shaft with her other hand and pulled on the velvety length. With each glide from base to tip, she enjoyed the electrifying sensations stimulating in her. His pleased moans reverberated in her like a magic spell.

"This could go much quicker if you just explained." She paused in her movement.

"I'm in no hurry."

His face wrinkled at the tickle of her finger just beneath the head of his cock. Lines of pleasure creased his face as she rubbed the small dip.

"Is this a sensitive place?" She laughed.

She leaned over and wiggled her tongue in the very same place. The warm-veined shaft throbbed erratically and she continued to torture just that one tiny sweet spot.

"Oh God." His groan rattled in his chest for a long time.

She slipped her lips over the tip and swirled her tongue under the rim several times. Lifting her eyes, she saw the intensity of his expression increase. She dragged her tongue up and down in long, slow strokes, licking the thin, soft skin until it quivered. Each time she pulled away, his erection stretched to reach her mouth.

Katerina caressed his rock-hard cock, inch by inch. From the firm, heart-shaped cap, to the base nested into a thick patch of black hair, she gave him everything. A loud slurping over his balls made him hum and rake the covers into his fists. She knew she had gained an advantage.

The musky male scent had her hungering to keep her nose against his body. It didn't matter where. He smelled good, wholesome and delectable.

She swirled her tongue back to the glistening tip of his cock and caught a crystal droplet of moisture. Another taste encouraged her to suck it deep into her throat. The scrumptious essence of him spurted into her swallows.

Katerina gulped every delicious drop. She lapped at the tip until she washed it away. In her excitement, she rained kisses on his groin and up over his shirt to his chest. He breathed heavily, irregularly, yet matched her pants to perfection.

She put her head down, resting against his heartbeat. His hand smoothed over her head and words eluded them both. For five minutes she wondered what he thought of her, what he would say when he did speak. In some ways she dreaded it. He had a sadistic way of torturing her with his indecisive feelings.

"What do you want to know?" He pressed a kiss on the top of her head.

She lifted her face and looked at him with a million questions in mind and only one she wanted answered.

"Will you reciprocate?"

Dax held Katerina firmly and, in an easy maneuver, rolled her onto her back. His fingers swept over her face and he stared at her with a feeling of pure happiness.

"All you ever have to do is ask." He lowered his head, kissing her.

Gently pulling her lips between his, he nipped her tongue and she licked his.

Dax worked her dress up high on her long legs and slid a hand under the hem. He found the nest of ringlets soft, wet and eagerly twisting around his grip. She wiggled as he dipped a finger to rub the hood of her clit. The soft skin stiffened as he rolled it with the pad of his thumb.

"Dax," she murmured, kissing his face wherever her lips landed.

"You enchant me with your freshness, Katerina. You have such a hard exterior, it's not easy to imagine the beautiful softness of your soul unless you're in my arms."

"You know how to touch me," she explained with a simplicity he accepted.

"Yes and you do a fine job at handling me as well."

"I don't know how to make you tell me things I wish to know."

He smiled and parted her nether lips wide to accept his middle finger.

She whimpered and her mouth trembled against his jaw.

"It hurts a little?" He already knew it did as he tested the resistance of her hymen by pushing deeper than he had before.

She nodded and buried her face against his neck. Her moist lips pressed against his skin and her lashes fluttered, tickling his earlobe.

He pushed deeper, unable to reach far enough to break the barrier. "Hold on to me as tight as you want."

He tried again and then backed off because it hurt her.

"When I'm inside you, the pain will come again." He felt he should explain. "You know this, don't you?"

"Yes." Her voice rushed out before her lips kissed his neck.

"I want to make love to you, Princess. I want to feel every ounce of the passion you try to hide. I want to pleasure you as no man ever has."

Her fingers rubbed over his chin, up his jaw and slid behind his ear. He slowly pumped his fingers in her wet cunt, making sure not to go as far as the blockade. With the pad of his thumb circling her clit, he kept her anxiously excited and distracted. She bestowed upon him kisses by the thousands, covering every heated pore in his skin.

"Dax," she hummed. "Dax, kiss me."

Her gentle voice begging for what he already wanted wasn't enough to satisfy him. She had to surrender herself completely. Between forefinger and thumb, he held her jaw. He licked over her lips and met her pink tongue licking back.

"You'll marry me?"

She nodded.

A sudden burp from her lips created hiccups to pop up. The crowberry wine puffed at his face.

"How much wine have you had?"

Her dreamy smile without words made him think she might be drunk.

"I don't know."

"A little alcohol and you're as tame as a kitten, aren't you?" He laughed.

"Make love to me."

"In due time, beautiful."

He covered her mouth, sealing off any more talk. Delightful sounds rumbled in her throat. Her hips lifted to his hand pumping and his fingers probing. He moved his kisses to her neck, to her lobe and he swirled the tip of his tongue around the delicate shell of her ear.

Her muted laugh and her squirming became more agitated.

"Dax," her sultry voice cooed.

"Shhh..."

"Oh please." Her fingers clawed and caught up a fistful of his hair.

He slithered down the length of her, spread her legs and forced the gown higher. Taking in her incredibly soft cunt in his mouth, he thrust his tongue, licking every crevice and every ounce of her sweet beauty. With a gentle nip to her clit, he tugged the knot of flesh.

"Oh, God that feels so good, Stefan," she panted.

Dax lifted his head and rose up over her.

"Open your eyes."

The long, dark lashes fluttered a few times.

"Who do you see?"

"Dax," she purred.

Her hand cupped his face and languidly stroked his cheek. Her inspection dipped a nail into his mouth. She rubbed his lips and his teeth.

"Do me again," she begged. "It wasn't enough."

"You've fooled me, Princess. I took for granted that your iciness meant you'd never given a man a taste of you."

"Taste me," she repeated with a giggle.

Dax crushed her lips with a tumultuous kiss. The very idea she had a memory of another man burned his lungs. His chest tightened and he wanted to kiss her so well she'd never speak another man's name again. His fingers moved over her gown to undress her. He'd do more than he knew any man had done. He'd bury his cock into her aching cunt and make her scream his name during her orgasm.

Dax took the hard nipple into his mouth and let his tongue roll over the bead, enjoying her soft fluttering moans. He pushed his hand over her quivering belly, rubbing his fingers between her thighs.

"Mmmm." She squirmed.

"I like that you're wet for me." He felt her juices flow. The dripping desire of her delicate folds drew his fingers in to explore.

"I know." She wiggled her hips to take in his probe. "Your arrogance has yet to fail you."

Dax laughed and plunged his middle finger up as far as he could reach. "Then let me not disappoint you now."

He hit the barrier inside her. The little grunt she made was a vain attempted to mask her discomfort. Her hand went to her mouth to stifle her sounds, yet they leaked out.

"Tell me you don't want this." He thrust faster into her wet center.

Her hand reached to his head and she tangled her fingers in his hair.

"Should I stop?" he teased.

"No, please, not yet."

He pulled his hand from her.

"Nooooo!"

At her frustrated cry, he slid down to cup his mouth over her blushing, hot cunt.

"Oh!" Katerina's voice chirped.

He sucked on her gush of heated fluids. He drank from her as her stuttered gasps bid him to do more.

She pulled at his head involuntarily. Apparently it stressed her not to know what to do. He knew, but didn't want to rush her. This moment was all about changing one stubborn lady into a sexual predator. He wanted her to become an aggressive partner. She neared her climactic peak and he eased back from letting her orgasm fully bloom. She tugged on his hair and her agitated nails dug into his scalp.

To hear her beg would be to his ultimate delight.

“Dax.”

Her fingers slid to his ears. She held them as if she had a grip on the reins of her steed. He reared up, leaving her cunt openly twitching. His cock hard, he didn’t know if he could resist her much longer. His balls tightened painfully.

The seductress seemed the winner of this foreplay.

“Please, Dax, I want you in me.” She reached a hand out to him.

He had the dubious victory of hearing her plead.

“Dax, please.”

He pushed a finger in her and felt her vagina ready to lay claim to anything.

“Is that all you wish to do?” she goaded. “Finger me?”

Her dreamy gaze, from half-closed eyes, taunted him. She stretched her arms over her head and writhed beneath his thrusting hand. Her orgasm drove her body into spasms.

“Oh God, please, Dax, please!”

He jerked his fingers from inside her and hurried to lower his unfastened trousers. It wasn’t fast enough. His cock swung out over Katerina and spurt the creamy fluid over her belly.

“Damn,” he grumbled.

He fell forward on his hands and let the massive tremors finish him off. His cock lay on her like some errant pipe while his spending drenched her.

He looked at her heavy breathing. Her pants of intoxicated exhaustion pushed her right into a deep sleep. Her peaceful repose brought him down low where he could kiss her.

"A funny thing happened on my way to seducing you." He chuckled. "I went and got too hot to hold back.

He claimed her mouth and kissed her slowing breath.

"Some things are meant to be, my beautiful princess, and you and I are one of them."

Dax crawled off the bed to fetch a rag to clean them both up from his premature ejaculation. If Katerina could make him that rushed when she was drunk, he couldn't wait to experience a full night of sexual abandonment with her.

Chapter Twenty-seven

When Katerina opened her eyes, the room had little light and she wondered how long she had slept. A headache prevented her from getting up right away. The pins were missing from her hair. The long tresses spread everywhere—across the pillow, down her arm, over Dax and under his face pressed into the pillow alongside her. Tugging carefully, she tried to liberate her hair. It slid a little and stopped. With just enough slack to rise, she looked over Dax. He slept on his stomach. He had her hair under him and wrapped in his hand.

Unable to think of a graceful way in which to get unbound, she poked him in the ribs.

"Ouch," Dax complained.

"Let go of my hair," she ordered. "If I'd known you were going to hang onto me all night, I would have let you sleep on the floor."

Dax propped himself up on an elbow, wound her hair tighter, making her move closer. His cool cerulean eyes regarded her with amusement. Excitement sang in her heart when his face neared.

"Me, hang on to you?" He chuckled. "You hugged me all night long like I was your pet dog."

"I didn't!"

He rolled his hand and her hair came free.

"I'll not argue, Princess. You may believe what you like." He dropped to his back. "Get ready to leave."

Memories of the night reclaimed her sanity. He had been marvelous, fulfilling many of her desires. Yet, she had trouble recalling the end to their union. The soreness inside her made her only too aware at how he must have used her. His magnificently broad chest expanded with his yawn. She thought how wonderful it would be to kiss him. Her tongue flicked over her lips to wet the morning dryness. She swallowed the staleness and decided maybe it was better they not lock their mouths together. It might lead him to want more of her.

"Come here." Dax on the other hand had different plans.

He pulled her down, his hand held the back of her head.

"Good morning, beautiful." He planted his mouth over hers and sucked at her lips. His other hand rubbed her back and ended up skittering over her gown to grip her ass.

"Dax, please." She gasped for air.

He had a way of surprising, exciting and stepping over bounds of decency. Her nipples tightened and she realized her bare breasts were touching his naked flesh.

"Begging me a little early, aren't you? As nice as that would be, we haven't time for me to pleasure you this morning."

She sat up with her back pressed to the wall. Her body heaved with memories of the night and she worked quickly at buttoning up the gown. She wanted to groan as she recalled begging him to make love to her.

With Dax in front of her, the only way off the bed was over him. She waited for him to get up. In the meanwhile, she searched the blankets for her hairpins. She didn't know how she'd get her hair gathered back in a semblance of decency without her lady's maid.

"You never said why I should go to Volda." She raked at her long hair trying to assemble it.

"To keep you and your brother safe."

"Balthazar will be going there as well?" She inched her dress up to crawl around on the bed.

"He'll meet us at the ship." He ran his finger down her nose.

Katerina sat still, not wanting to offer up any more of her affections. His finger continued outlining her jaw, brushing her bottom lip and dropping from her chin to her chest.

She shivered with the weakness of exhilaration. He gave a laugh and she slapped his hand away.

Dax got up, added wood to the fire and scooped up a bowl of stew. She didn't like his watchful stare as he ate. Trying to ignore him, she wrestled with the long, thick locks draped over her shoulders and hanging as far as her waist.

"If I were a little braver, I would chop this mane off."

She twisted, pulled and coiled her hair up. Only it didn't all cooperate.

"You'll not cut it off because I like it." He set the bowl down and walked to her. Reaching around her waist, he dragged her to him. "Sit still."

He gathered her hair in one hand. His fingers combed over it, caressing her neck inadvertently. It made bumps rise on her skin. He separated her hair into three long hanks and with gentle tugs, plaited the coils into a neat and tidy braid.

When he flipped it over her shoulder, she looked at the white silk cravat tied on the end. Her skin dampened, she felt wet between her legs and her examination of the silk went on far too long. Dax had to comment.

"I remember the night as well." He pressed a kiss to the side of her neck.

She tried to pull away. He didn't give her the satisfaction and she found her mouth against his.

"Don't resist, Princess. You'll be sorry you missed out. I might not offer this opportunity again for quite a while."

She pushed his hand away, embarrassed by his teasing. "I won't be sorry for anything, especially your unwanted attention."

Katerina swung her legs off the bed and tried standing. Without boots on her feet, she stepped on the hem of her dress and tripped. She landed on the floor with a firm thud.

"Your Highness." Dax held his hand out.

She looked at his long fingers, his open palm and the tiny scar on his thumb. She felt a curious need to ask how he got it. Shoving his hand aside, she got up from the floor on her own and retrieved her boots from near the fireplace.

"When do we leave?" She helped herself to the food and wrinkled her nose at the lukewarm concoction. A few bites and she slid the bowl away.

"Whenever you're ready, Princess."

"I want to go now." She put her coat on and bundled it tight with the tie.

"As you command." He broke off a piece of bread and stuffed it in his mouth before donning his own heavy sheepskin coat.

Chapter Twenty-eight

The sleigh was small and packed tight. Dax held Katerina's arm while she climbed in. He made several checks of the horse, harness and the supplies. Joining her, he sat and squished her in the narrow space.

"Something more comfortable could have been found." She jerked her coat wedged between them.

"Like your throne?" Dax stood releasing her coat from under his weight. He pulled her up, sat and then tugged her down so she sat on his coat. "I find this quite cozy and we'll stay warmer."

He snapped the reins and the sleigh took off behind the horse. They traveled an hour in brittle silence. The fog stayed as thick as mutton stew. The journey went slow. The mountains looming in the east remained mere shadows against the diffused sky.

Katerina sighed while looking at the rumbling mountain. Dax knew what she prayed for, just as he did. No one wanted the massive volcano to erupt. There were a number of them on the Aleutian Islands and they connected. If one spewed molten lava, it could set off a chain reaction. His home didn't stand a chance of surviving its volcano's disturbance.

With the smell of ash permeating the air, the burnt stench belched from the bowels of the earth. Every year, a couple of the islands of the Aleutian Sea trembled with earthquakes. Every few decades, one or two erupted. In the past century, two islands had become uninhabitable. One day, it could be his very own home of Volda.

"We'll not be here if it erupts," he told her.

"I sometimes think when it does, it will be bigger than we ever imagined and cover my whole kingdom in blackened rock. You know, where one boils with the fires of hell, so do others. It may be something no one escapes."

"I'm very aware of that, Princess."

As soon as he smelled the first traces of the charring scent, he thought of nothing else. "Does it rumble often?"

"Every couple of years it fills the sky with ash. It appears like a fine snow, only gray, dirty and stinky."

"Nothing major then?"

"Not for more than two hundred years." She tried shifting on the seat.

"Let's hope it has no wish to do more for the next two hundred years as well."

"My bottom is numb, my feet are cold and I think my fingers could crack off like icicles. Can't we stop and get warm or are you intent on delivering me to my brother as a block of ice?"

He wondered if fear made her irritable. He stopped the sleigh and looked at her holding her hood shut. Inside the dome of fur, Katerina huffed and puffed in an effort to warm her face.

"Give me your hands." He pulled one from her grip on the hood.

"Why? What are you going to do?"

"Why, I think I'll snap off your pretty little fingers and dispose of them." He tugged her glove off. "Warm your hands, of course. Now give me the other hand."

She did as he asked. He removed the glove and looked at her bright red fingers.

"Put one under each of my arms." He opened his coat.

Her hands drifted toward him. She gently placed them on his ribs forcing him to laugh.

She withdrew.

"I'm sorry, Princess."

"I don't find this funny." She blew her breath on her hands and rubbed them together.

"Here." He took a hand and put it under his arm. "I wasn't laughing at you. I'm a bit ticklish in the ribs and you were touching too lightly."

"Oh." She blushed.

He held his other arm up and she slid her fingers into place.

"Now come close to me." He pulled her into the opening of his coat.

He watched her avoid looking at him. The fog dispersed with the rise of the sun. The shimmer of light bounced off the falling snowflakes. He saw it attracted her attention. When she lifted her lashes, he caught her gaze.

Katerina's hood fell back. A cold breeze pulled at her hair and he tugged the fur back into place. He had a dozen plans tumbling in his mind. Which one would work most to his advantage was the one he'd have to choose.

Dax held her head and covered her mouth with his own. She moved her cold lips, teasing his in response. When she sighed, he eased his tongue through the opening. Her small puffs of ardor warmed him. She heated his blood with the memories of the night before. It wasn't the time to start something he couldn't finish and yet he couldn't stop as long as she submitted to him.

He sucked on her tongue, savoring the taste of her. She took a turn at doing the same and her soft moan expressed her pleasure.

He drew his head back and looked at her wondrous stare. The stardust in her eyes ensnared him. It made him forget he had to wait until things were settled with Talbot before he ventured into plans already made.

"Are your fingers warm enough? We need to keep going." He purposely spoke with indifference. The last thing he needed was for her to think she could manipulate him.

"No, but don't let me hinder this trip." She yanked her hands out from under his arms.

"You'll get warm when you're on my ship." He handed her the gloves and drove the horse.

"I still think we should go back to the castle. Question all the guards and ferret out the dastardly culprit." She stomped her feet.

"You needn't have a tantrum."

"If you don't mind, my feet are cold. I was trying to get circulation back in my toes. Now I order you to take me back to the castle. I don't want to leave Alluvia."

"Sorry, no. This is one wish I cannot grant."

"You do recall this is my kingdom and I'm in charge, don't you?" She held her hood to the side, looking over at him. "You only get to do what I allow."

"If you say so."

"I do say so. You must obey me. It is only right that as a guest of my land you act upon my command."

"You'll do as I say if you'd like to stay alive."

He snapped the reins harder and the horse galloped through the snow. It hit a rock or a rut and Katerina went flying forward. He grabbed her before she exited the cart, and he pulled her back into his lap.

"You could have killed me." She pried his fingers from her waist.

The thick wool coat didn't give him the leverage to hold on and she climbed out of the sleigh and fell in the snow.

"Katerina! Katerina come back. There's no place to go and you'll freeze to death."

"Stay away from me, you lunatic." She kept walking in the path where the blade of the sleigh had cut through the powdery snow.

"Come back, Princess. This will get you nowhere. Another fifteen or twenty minutes and we'll be over the rise to where the port is with my ship."

"Then what?" She dropped down to sit in the snow. "My feet are frostbitten, my hands are like ice and you won't give me a straight answer about anything. For all I know, you want me dead."

"You think that, after all we've done together?" Dax hunched down in front of her. "Did I kiss you like harming you was ever my intention?"

"How should I know how you think? Maybe you're crazy."

"You are for sitting in the snow. Your bottom will join ranks with your fingers and toes and also get numb if you stay there."

She looked up at him.

"I know the past couple days have been eventful, but I assure you, I would never do a thing to hurt you." Dax scooped her up and she held onto him. "It won't be long before I have you out of this weather."

"And then you'll go back to being mean to me again."

"Maybe not as much as you think."

The snow fell heavier, making it harder to see. The mountains to the east disappeared. Soon, the advancing blizzard would make travel hard on land.

Dax felt Katerina hug tight and his heart hugged along with his arms. He trudged through the snow to the sleigh and sat her on the seat. From the back, he retrieved a satchel and unwrapped the bundle containing food and a jug.

"Drink this. It'll help warm you." He pulled the cork and tipped the jug to her chattering teeth.

She lifted her hand and placed it over his to steady the container.

"Vodka," she whispered after the first sip.

He saw the immediate effects of warmth engulf her as the liquid poured in and she took swallow after swallow.

"Easy, Princess, you've not eaten enough today to drink this like water." He took the jug away and took a large gulp for himself.

"I can handle drinking liquor."

"Like last night, I suppose."

She pursed her lips in obvious annoyance.

Dax took another drink, letting barely a drop touch his tongue. It shot to the back of his throat and left a fiery trail to the pit of his stomach. Katerina had that same affect when she looked at him. She made him tingle all over with a flurry of mysterious anticipation. Controlling his emotions proved hard when he had her within reach.

"My feet are still cold. If you hadn't decided to abduct me, I'd be toasty warm at home."

"I'll see to you getting your comfort once we're on the ship." He handed her a loaf of bread. "Eat this."

They set off again and Dax took more care with the horse and sleigh.

The snow came heavier. He thought spring had finally chased off the worst of winter, but the dense flurries proved him wrong.

"I can't see anything. How do you know we're going the right way?"

"A sense of direction."

Katerina ate half the loaf. She hiccupped and he turned his head, not letting her see the grin on his face.

"You should eat too." She broke a chunk off the loaf and put the bite-sized piece to his lips.

He looked at the gloved fingers.

"Well?" She waited.

He opened his mouth and she stuck the bread inside. She smiled with a childish delight.

"Do you wish to say something?" He observed the cocoa eyes fixated on his mouth.

Her inebriated expression filled with confusion. Then her head bobbed a couple times and promptly fell forward on his arm.

"Or maybe you'd rather pass out." He positioned his arm in front of her to keep her back in the seat.

Chapter Twenty-nine

The ship stood ready to sail. Atop the main mast, the violet and green flag flapped in the wind. The storm threatened but never hit them. The vibrant colors of Dax's home waved him on and he snapped the reins one last time to speed up the horses.

Passed out, Katerina slept against him. With her face burrowed in the fur of his coat and her arms snaked in a tight hold around his, he drove them to the docks.

"Your Highness, I have brought you to safety," he whispered as he stopped the horses at their destination.

Dax climbed down, holding her in place. She sat slouched in the seat, unaware of everything. He pulled his glove off and touched the back of his curled finger to her bright red cheek.

"While our plans are far apart at the moment, I'll see no harm is ever done to you. This I promise on my life. You're safe with me, my sweet Katerina."

"I know," she muttered in her semiconscious state.

He smiled and picked her up.

"You don't do well on alcohol, Princess."

Her dark lashes lifted and she gazed at him with attractively ignorant bliss.

“I rarely drink wine.” She hiccupped and laughed. “Gives me a headache and I have enough of those without adding to the problem.”

She laid her head on his shoulder. Noisily yawning, she snuggled her face into the fur of his hood. “I’m cold and tired. Can we go to bed now?”

“Certainly, beautiful.”

The men onboard his ship bowed as he carried Katerina aboard.

“Your Highness,” they greeted.

“They know who I am just like that woman.” She looked up at him with a dreamy yet smug stare. “You thought people wouldn’t recognize me.”

“Forgive my blunder.”

“They’ll obey my orders if you don’t.”

“We’ll discuss that later.” Dax kissed her forehead.

“Everything is later with you.” She pushed her lips to his and kissed him. “I want you now.”

Dax smiled, finding her change of topic intriguing. When he looked up, he saw Giselle rushing across the deck toward him. Her small fur-clad form was even graceful under the cumbersome coat.

“Dax, what took you so long? I didn’t think you’d ever get here. The weather has been miserable and I was afraid you’d not make it.”

“I’m here now. Did you have any problems with the prince?”

“No. He’s agreed to stay put because he believed me when I told him you were bringing the princess here.”

Katerina dusted her gloved hand over his face.

"What's wrong with her?" Giselle asked.

"She's drunk."

"I won't ask how, but I suggest we get her in the cabin." Giselle put a hand to his arm. "It's cold out here."

"She'll be fine. The warm effects of vodka make her unaware of the cold."

"I wouldn't think she'd drink so much under the circumstances."

"She hardly ate yesterday or today. She did, however, consume a considerable amount of liquor. Once the results wear off, I'm sure to get an earful."

"Speaking of which, I've put Prince Balthazar in my cabin." Giselle's worried eyes glistened. "He's been demanding answers. I think he suspects something is going on besides what happened on the cliffs. What will you tell him?"

"I suppose the truth." He walked toward the passage leading to the cabins below deck.

"He'll be furious."

"It won't matter. There's nothing he can do to change things." He ducked under the beam and followed the passage to the last door.

"I'll be so glad when we're home and this is all over."

"So will I, Giselle."

Dax stopped in front of his door just as Prince Balthazar emerged from Giselle's cabin.

"Kat!" The prince quickly came forward and put an arm up preventing Dax from taking Katerina into the room. "What's happened to her?"

"Vodka, Your Highness. I gave her some to keep her blood from freezing and she's intoxicated." He wished he could think of something other than what he was about to say to them, but he couldn't.

Katerina picked up her head and looked at the prince. "We're going to bed now, Balthazar." She smiled wanly. "Dax promised."

"I insist you tell me what's going on." The prince glared at him.

"I'll explain all if you'll let me get the princess into bed and warmed up."

Prince Balthazar stepped aside.

The small coal stove had the room exceptionally toasty. Dax placed Katerina on the bunk and pulled her arms free. She looked up at him with a puzzled, yet adoring gaze. He wanted to kiss her but rejected the idea because of her brother's presence.

"Giselle, please see to princess," Dax instructed.

He motioned for Balthazar to follow him. Taking the prince down the passage, he opened a door that placed them in another cabin—a small, modest room for guests. He had Giselle give her cabin and his to the guests for their comfort.

The coal stove had not been lit and Dax stooped down to do the job himself. The bitter cold made him ache clean through to his bones. He rubbed his hands in front of the small flame of paper he used to start the fire.

"Well?" The prince's boot tapped the floor with impatience.

"One moment." He went up on deck and found his ship's commander.

The man stood rigid and in dire need of a job to do after hanging around in stables waiting for Dax to decide just when he would leave port.

The ship's captain, Junroe, gave Dax a knowing grin from atop the quarterdeck, understanding Dax's nod meant they were to set sail.

"Take up the anchor," Junroe shouted as Dax turned back to the prince behind him in the passageway.

"Was that an order to sail?" The prince's face reddened with rage.

"Yes, Your Highness, it was. We're destined for Volda if Giselle hasn't told you." Dax squeezed past the prince and returned the heated room.

"No, she hasn't said anything. She's an apt student when it comes to deceit. You've trained her very well to avoid important topics."

"Giselle has her reasons for doing what she must, as do I."

"I have no wish to leave Alluvia. Actually it is imperative that my sister and I remain here."

"I'm sorry, Your Highness. That doesn't work with my plans. I insist you visit Volda for a short while. At the end of the month, you will be returned to your palace." Dax stirred the coals and closed the grate.

"We're being abducted!"

"Think of it as an unplanned trip."

Dax turned away and busied himself with undressing. To be out of his wet, borrowed clothes and into something dry grew urgent. The warmth would pick his up spirits.

"You'll let me and my sister off this ship at once. I am the prince regent of this kingdom and soon to be king. I command you to obey me."

"You and your sister do think alike. I hate to inform you, but once on this vessel, you came under the laws of Volda and only the king can grant your wishes." Dax chuckled and stood naked in front of the stove. "And that, I'm afraid, he cannot do at the present time."

"Why is that? the prince demanded.

"It just comes with my position." Dax pulled on fresh breeches and a thick pair of woolen socks.

"The king has sent you to do this, why?"

"Something we'll speak of at another time."

"I must be in Alluvia and marry before the end of the month."

"I can guarantee you this, Your Highness. You will miss that date." Dax pulled a shirt over his head and tied it closed. He stuck an arm in a vest and fastened it as well.

"My uncle, Lord Talbot, has set this whole thing up, hasn't he?"

"Yes, Lord Talbot is the puppet master at the present time."

"Puppet master? Then you don't do this willingly?" The prince stopped his pacing. "What is it, money or lands? I'll pay more."

"I do this under duress and I hope you will forgive me in the future, but I'll understand if you cannot." He opened the door. "Now if you'd like to spend some time with your sister and assure her you're safe, I would appreciate your cooperation. The princess was very worried and I wouldn't want to deprive her of your sobering stare."

"I could have you executed for this treachery." Balthazar narrowed his eyes. He brushed past Dax and took long, quick strides to Katerina's cabin.

Giselle bowed her head and moved back from the bed. Dax pulled her alongside him. Tears glistened in her eyes. His plot caused her distress, but he couldn't have done anything differently. Prince Balthazar's disregard of her made the situation worse. Highly emotional and sensitive, his sister didn't have a strong, forceful personally like Katerina.

"Kat?" The prince held his sister's hand. "Kat, wake up and listen to me."

She groaned in protest and rolled over. Her eyes opened and stared blankly at the prince.

"Balthazar I have another one of my headaches. Would you be a dear and get me something."

"Katerina, listen to me. This is important."

"Nothing is important when I have one of these headaches." She put a hand over her eyes. "It's worse than ever."

"The vodka will do that to you," Dax informed her.

Chapter Thirty

Katerina lifted her head and looked at Dax. Her quick movement came with a painful stab of pressure behind her eyes and it forced her back on the downy pillow.

"What did you do to me?" she demanded, in tears.

Her memory slipped in and out of things said and things that happened. Fantasy and reality intertwined.

"I kept you from freezing to death, Your Highness," Dax answered.

"We've been kidnapped." Balthazar rubbed her temples. "It would seem we were duped by this fellow and his sister, if that's who Giselle really is." He spit her name out harshly.

Giselle rushed from the cabin and Katerina felt the young woman's angst with an empathetic glance at the pain on Dax's face.

"My sister has never been shown the slightest disdain for anything. I warn you not to make another harsh comment about her."

Katerina struggled to sit up and show strength, even though she felt weak like a newborn lamb.

"Princess, if you're satisfied that your brother is safe, I'll have to ask him to leave us now," Dax told her.

"Why can't we stay together?"

"I'll permit him to visit you from time to time and vice versa, but the two of you cannot be allowed to speak alone, lest I think you plot against me." He put a hand to the door and held it as Balthazar stood next to her.

"You'll keep us locked apart knowing we have no escape on these icy waters?"

"No, not locked up, Your Highness. I do not see either of you plunging into the depths of the Bering Sea to die. You are both permitted to wander about freely, just not together, unless my sister or I are with you. There will be one of my crew members in the passageway, keeping an eye on you."

"Just what I wanted, the company of you or your sister."

"I do believe you will have to rely on my time. Giselle will keep her distance after your harsh words. She is only doing as I say and I would deem it a kindness on your part not to blame her so severely."

"Nevertheless, she has played a part in all this," Balthazar grunted.

"Go on, Balthazar, I'll be all right." Katerina sat on the edge of the bunk. She refrained from standing since she felt lightheaded.

The silence lasted long after Balthazar left the room.

"Are we prisoners?" She pressed fingers to her eyes, wishing she had ice water with rose petals, just as her lady's maid had brought for her.

"Not exactly. Let's call you guests of Volda." He spread his legs slightly, standing at ease. "It will not be for long and no harm will come to you or your brother as long as you behave."

"Behave." Her outrage helped hoist her off the bunk. "You hypocritical barbarian."

She swung her hand and missed him. Swaying with a light head, she twisted from Dax's attempt to grab her and swung again. Her hand slapped him soundly across the cheek. She staggered back with a gasp.

"Good shot, Your Highness. I'll allow that one." He pulled her hand from her mouth and placed her palm against his hot cheek. "You wound me, Princess, when I've promised to not let any harm come to you."

She tugged at her hand. "Let go this instant." She lifted her other hand and found it a mistake.

Dax had both her hands pressed to his face and he lowered his head. "This is how lovers start a kiss," he whispered, drawing her hands behind his head and bringing her face closer, her body leaning upon his.

"I'll not kiss a self-centered cretin merely because of an attraction I have for you." She held her breath for the error in divulging the thought.

"Oh, Princess, how easily you forget how our lips touched places unspeakable for strangers. I'll freely admit I am attracted to you."

He put his face too close and while she desired his kiss, she didn't find pleasure in it being forced upon her. Or she hadn't thought she would until his delicious mouth covered hers. His heated breath rushed into her lungs.

Katerina struggled to free her arms from his grasp. He let go and drew her in tighter, allowing her to mold against his solid body. Stroking the back of his head with her fingers, she hungrily participated in the kiss, aggressive with her need to taste him. His passion rose to meet hers and his kisses attacked her mouth.

"Katerina." He whispered her name and it eased her troubled mind.

Pressing fingertips to his moist lips, she kissed along his jaw and beneath his chin. Sucking the warm, pulsing vein in his neck, she gave him a bruising love bite.

Keeping Dax off guard would work only if she put her whole body into the ploy. Rubbing against him and purring like a kitten, her mind labored over ideas of how to get off Dax's ship. She didn't want to leave him, but she hadn't a clue what unscrupulous plans he had plotted.

"Very nice presentation, Your Highness." He framed her face in his hands. "Now that I can see you have no problem with pretending, I ask that you sit and listen to my proposition."

Katerina silently fumed. Never had a man been so pleasantly harassing. He had seen that the heart she put into her actions had ulterior motives.

"You will be my betrothed." He held a hand up to stop her from speaking. "Listen and then you can ask questions. Your uncle wishes to have your kingdom and I am his means. His intentions for me, as well as Giselle, are to preoccupy you and your brother. We're to divert your attention from marrying anyone else."

"Why would you do this?"

"That we'll discuss once we reach Volda."

"And the shooting?"

"I had nothing to do with the shooting yesterday, but if I may offer a scenario, I believe Lord Talbot would find it advantageous to have you and the prince killed."

"How would he explain?"

"I would be his pawn. Blame would fall on me and he would dispose of you and me in the same plot to get control of Alluvia."

"What hold does he have over you?" She couldn't resist reaching out and touching his hand, sliding her fingers over the back of his knuckles in a soothing manner.

"Let's say, I value my life."

"How can marrying me work to your favor?" She stopped stroking him, waiting for him to reaffirm his intentions.

"I'm not really going to marry you." He turned his palm up where she felt the heat of his pulse. "We visit Lord Talbot with our news. He wanted me to keep you from looking for another to be your husband. I'll explain to him that at the last minute, I will rescind the contract with you."

"And let him have my crown." She jerked her hand from his in frustration.

"It would keep your brother safe."

"Why can't you marry me and thwart his plans altogether?" She rubbed her temples, not sure she could believe what she just asked of her kidnapper.

His grin sent a shudder through her.

"Why must we be taken away from Alluvia?"

"Lord Talbot only needed me to prevent you and your brother from marrying. However, he didn't specify how I would do that. Therefore your voyage to Volda is not his plan, but mine."

"Why would he think I'd marry you? Some lord of another land when I have my pick of thousands?"

"Come, Katerina. We all know that was the reason for the ball, the invitations to lands far away. You don't want just any man, do you?" He knelt down in front of her. "I would think you'd not settle for less than the fairytale of a handsome, strong and devoted man."

"None of that has a place in ruling a country. Of course you would not know of such things, seeing you only follow the orders of your king."

"That's a shame because the king might take an interest in you, and while I'm not up on a woman's fancies, Giselle informs me the king fits those very qualities which you seek."

"I told you I'm in need of a husband, bound by contract and nothing more." She stiffened as he touched her leg. The brocade offered no protection against the pressure of his fingers massaging her thigh. "I only need...stop doing that."

"You truly are beautiful." He folded an arm around her back as he rose up from his crouched position and brought her to her feet. "I should like to kiss you."

"You wouldn't dare. Not after what you've told me." Her arms, already in the air from rubbing her temples to dispel the headache, remained up and ready to strike, when all of a sudden he let go.

"You're right. I shall wait until you beg me to kiss you."

"You arrogant, puffed-up penguin."

"Maybe I should hold out for you to be on your knees pleading for my touch."

"Don't hold your breath. You think, because you have eyes the color of my royal gems, I'd hunger to add you to my cache of valuables?"

"Not exactly. I was thinking because I'd guard your virtue."

"You mock me. I'm not a pampered child."

He caught her chin and held her face.

"You're a foolish, overindulged woman who let an important matter go until the last minute. You and your brother have not given enough thought to your people's welfare."

"That's not true. You don't know me or Balthazar. You don't know our devotion to our country or the magnitude of our problems."

"'I know your father was foolish to force such an action on you and the prince." He let go of her and walked to a cabinet. "Flaws such as these allow the enemy to get the upper hand."

"If Lord Talbot thought his plan would work with you and Giselle, why would he try to kill Balthazar?"

"I don't know. Maybe his plan is not the same as he laid out to me." Dax took out blankets and sat them on a chair.

"I'll have to discuss this with my brother."

"No discussions of any sort can be done outside of us knowing. It puts your brother at risk."

"And me?"

"Lord Talbot seems to regard you as a minor threat. His lack of good judgment will be his downfall."

"Oh? How is that?"

"I see you as a stronger adversary than your brother. You pick up on things least noticed. And you, my dear, are tricky."

"Some compliment. How do I explain to my brother my sudden infatuation with you?"

"After that kiss, I think you will have no problem in creating whatever lies you wish him to believe for his safety."

"If you think my kissing you will distract my brother..."

"I was going to suggest you tell him that in an effort to thwart Lord Talbot, you will marry me."

Katerina watched him open a trunk and lift out a casket to take with him.

"You said you wouldn't." She took a deep breath. "This plot of yours is very confusing."

He'd given her a lot to consider. Her headache made it hard to focus.

"Think about it, Your Highness. Devise your own plans and then come see me."

Dax left her with the deluge of ideas. Everyone had an agenda. The ideal solution from her viewpoint was to marry Dax. His proposition of pretending would suffice until she could convince him to really marry her.

Chapter Thirty-one

As Giselle made her opinion known, Dax warmed himself in front of the wood burner in his new cabin.

"You've made it so he hates me," Giselle wailed.

"He'll get over it and, if not, then he wasn't meant for you." Dax reached for the jug of vodka.

"Can't I tell him anything?" She paced the cabin, fidgeting with the fringe of her shawl.

"No. There is much I don't want the prince to know and you might make a mistake. Besides, I have made a few changes. After that shooting incident, I've a suspicion the prince and princess of Alluvia are not the only monarchs Lord Talbot plans to dispose of."

"Us? He would kill us as well?" She stopped and stared in disbelief.

"Yes. I had that feeling when he first proposed this charade. Unfortunately, we had no choice but to go along and pretend to believe he'd leave Volda out of this mess."

"What will we do?"

"Lord Talbot doesn't know me well enough to assume I'm a bumbling idiot." He held his hand to her. "I'll do my best to see we finish this with a happy ending. You and I deserve to be happy and so do our people."

"Have you told her you're the king of Volda?"

Dax smiled. "Not yet. It's nice to not have to play that role for a while."

"At least she still talks to you. Balthazar refuses to even look at me."

"Give him time to cool down, Giselle. We've put them in a precarious situation without their permission. He needs time to absorb that what we're doing will benefit him." His attention turned to the knock at the door. "Come in."

The door opened and Katerina remained in the corridor.

"Giselle would you mind leaving Princess Katerina and myself alone? I believe she's come to a decision about a proposal I made."

Giselle bowed her head and gave a slight curtsey on her way out.

"She doesn't look well." Katerina entered.

"She's not used to voyages and there's the stress I've placed on her in this matter. I'm afraid she's grown too fond of the prince."

"Oh, and it would be so horrible to have them in love?"

"Not if he returns her feelings. My sister is young, impressionable and resilient where it comes to her duties. She'll fair well when this is over, if nothing more than for my sake."

"Oh yes. Who should hope to have their own life if it isn't as your servant?" Katerina fingered the small wooden casket he had taken from the trunk in her cabin.

Dax picked up her hand. "That is private." He held her fingers up close to his face and slowly put them on his lips. "However, you may inspect all other objects in this cabin at your leisure."

She brushed her fingernail over his top lip. He knew the art of seduction was as foreign as the lands he took her to, but he wasn't immune to the way she exuded beauty. Inside and out, there was everything to like about her.

"I suppose I should be grateful to you for making a plan that would ensure the well-being of my brother and me. Without you, he might be dead. I guess there is no choice for me except to go along with your scheme."

"Good." Dax gripped her waist and firmly pushed her away. "I'm glad to hear you understand the gravity of the situation."

"Of course, I understand it. I simply don't like the way I'm being manipulated. Nevertheless, I suppose our lives are more important than who rules Alluvia." She glided about the room and took up his offer to inspect other things.

Dax narrowed his eyes. She plotted poorly but, nonetheless, Princess Katerina of Alluvia had reached a strategy that allowed her to pretend she would marry him and he approved of the end result.

"Now that we have settled that question, what say you turn in for the night? I myself could use a good night's sleep and..." His brow rose as she climbed on the bunk. "What are you doing?"

"You wish to sleep and I should like to watch." She pulled at the buttons on her coat. One button didn't like her abuse and popped completely off, skittering across the floor.

"Watch? What do you mean watch?"

His chest expanded with the breath he couldn't let out as she twisted and turned to shuck the garment off.

"I want to see how peaceful a devil can sleep if his captive is awake." She tugged her boots off and wiggled her irresistible toes. "Besides, you said you'd warm my feet and you have yet to do that."

She held a foot to him. The milky skin ended at her ankles and changed to an angry red glow over her chafed flesh. He took her foot in his hands.

"You want me to warm your feet?" He massaged the delicate arch with his thumbs. "Then you wish to watch me sleep?"

"Uh-huh."

She lay down and put her other foot up and rubbed it on the front of his shirt.

"Oh, that feels good." She closed her eyes and Dax kissed the bottom of her foot, first the heel, then the instep. He moved up to her damp wrinkled toes. The long entrapment in the boot left them soft. He sucked each toe into his mouth and he forced her to look up at him.

"Maybe I should go to the other cabin. You'll not get any sleep with me here," she said nervously, scooting back and removing her foot from his grasp.

"I think not as well. Though, staying awake for such things that would pleasure us both isn't always a bad notion." He grabbed her arms and pushed her back on the bunk. "This is why you wanted to stay, is it not?"

Katerina shook her head.

"That's too bad." He let go and stretched out on the bunk. "I hoped you were ready to beg me to make love to you."

"I never beg."

"Well go on then, run to the other cabin and leave me to sleep."

"I'll not run either. I'm not afraid of you." She sat in the corner of the bunk with her back pressed to the wall.

He stretched out on the mattress and, amazingly, Katerina did what he knew she wanted to do. She lay down alongside him, placed her head on his shoulder and a hand on his stomach.

Pleased, he closed his eyes.

“Comfortable?” He grazed her forehead with his lips.

“Yes, thank you.” Her finger swirled contemplatively over his chest. “Are we really headed for Volda?”

“Yes and you’ll find it very much like Alluvia.”

“Dax, I won’t beg, but I...I wouldn’t mind if you kissed me.”

“I suppose since you have agreed to be my betrothed, I could be lenient on the kissing part. After all, you will have to pretend to be infatuated with me. Practice is always beneficial.” He lifted her chin and twisted his mouth to fit hers.

Excitement crept in with her sigh and gave him an encouraging thrill. He kissed her with the gentle passion of a chaste lover, knowing she desired more. He pulled her restless body further on him. Her smooth, agitated fingers held his jaw, glided up behind his ears, twirled into his hair and tugged him into a kiss to end all time.

Dax parted her lips gently and slid his tongue into the cavern. He explored her mouth and reveled in the fact she was open with her passion. Her returned thrusts were amorous and appreciated. However, he couldn’t refrain from commenting.

“Aggressive even in bed, aren’t you, Your Highness,” he teased. “You fooled me well.”

“No talking,” she demanded.

“Always the ruler.” He rolled her over on her back. “Although, if you hadn’t noticed I don’t take orders, I give them.” He breathed his exhilaration into her open mouth.

“Uh-huh.”

Dax kissed her face, her jaw and moved along the silky column of her neck. He nibbled at her delicate earlobe and slid his tongue along the rim of her ear.

"I want you," he whispered, kissing a trail back to her sweet lips.

She didn't answer, but the little catches in her breath were not protests. Instead she gave him surrendering whimpers. He worked as fervently with his hands as he did with his mouth and got a hand inside her gown.

"Dax..."

"Shhh, no talking remember?" He licked her collarbone and journeyed downward to the breast he cupped in his hand.

"Dax you can't—"

His tongue glided over the tip and cut off her objection. She moaned with urgency and he pressed his mouth to the erect nipple waiting for him. She frantically sought solace in his arms while he steadily bathed the soft, rosy peak. From his attention, the spire hardened and Katerina softened in response.

She arched, offering more. Her head twisted to the side and her hands rubbed his shoulders.

"God you taste delicious." He lifted his head from her bosom and kissed her trembling lips.

"I think it's the vodka I spilled on myself." She giggled and he heard an innocent vulnerability in the sound.

"Yes, you might be right." He pulled the gown closed and fastened the buttons back in place. "Let's get some sleep."

"But—" She made an annoyed grunt.

Dax stared up at the planked ceiling, leaving Katerina stupified by his retreat.

She turned to her side, putting her back to him.

"I thought you wanted some warmth?" He moved over and put his hand on the curve of her hip.

"I think I'd rather seek it elsewhere." She gathered up her coat.

"Leaving so soon? I've not slept yet so you could watch," he teased unmercifully. "Are you upset that I'll not bed you...eventually?"

"If you mean again. You'll never get that pleasure." She climbed over him and off the bed.

"My sweet, you passed out and I never finished the first time. You're still very much a virgin."

Katerina's face reddened. She picked up her boots and stormed out of his cabin.

Chapter Thirty-two

It didn't surprise Katerina to see Giselle lingering in the corridor near Balthazar's cabin. As much as she tried to dislike the girl, she did seem innocent at times. Giselle's watery glance gave away emotions she couldn't hide and her cheeks flamed red with mortification for being caught.

Embarrassed by her own assumption that Dax had made love to her, even though she hadn't remembered details past a certain point, Katerina felt pity for Giselle.

"Your Highness." Giselle gave a bow of her head as she moved along pretending to head somewhere.

Ignoring Giselle's glance at the boots in her hand, Katerina took the girl's arm and towed her to Balthazar's door. She knocked and the door opened almost immediately. The room fanned out a wave of heat and she looked past the guard.

"You two need to talk, Balthazar." Katerina thrust the girl in before her since the guard appeared ready to make a protest of her entrance.

The guard stepped back for Giselle.

"I have no desire to talk to a conspirator." Balthazar turned his back on them.

"Please, Princess, let me go." Giselle's tears fell freely.

"No. You two need to speak," Katerina commanded while eyeing the guard with a warning not to get involved. "Balthazar, there is no need to hold a grudge. She's not the brains behind our captivity. Do not fault her because, if I am any judge of character, this lady would not cause you grief needlessly."

"What should we talk about?" He glanced back with a murderous glare at Giselle. Katerina waited for him to observe the sadness in the girl's expression. When the lines in his face softened, the kindness in him emerged. She knew her brother. His hurt would be no different then hers, but his loving soul needed to be pushed in the right direction at times. Cleverness was not always his strongest characteristic.

Katerina let go of Giselle's arm and went to Balthazar before the guard could stop her.

"Sweetness," she whispered quickly in his ear so only he could hear. "Be nice and see what you can learn from her. It may be our salvation, dear brother."

She twirled from him and headed out the door.

"Kat," Balthazar called to her. "Why haven't you got your boots on?"

Flustered, she didn't glance back. "I...I was hot."

Katerina pulled the door shut and ran down the passageway to her cabin. Another crewman watched her and she hurried to get behind the door and be alone.

Leaning on the back of the door for a moment, she viewed the room with a different perspective. The ornate moldings, the gilded artistry displayed wealth. The clothing in the drawers and trunks were obviously Dax's, she'd seen him go through them.

His room held information and gazing at the desk, she went to it in search of clues about his plans and the hold her uncle had over such a small country.

She pulled open a drawer and flipped through papers. Maps and notes, nothing of importance lay inside.

A flash of light outside the window caught her eye. The black heavens lit up the sky again with a jagged spear of electricity darting into the sea. The loud crack of thunder set her back in surprise. She steeled her nerves against the next rattling boom but the thunderous bang of the door spun her around.

"I couldn't sleep." Dax leaned on the doorframe.

He looked strange and a small notion the storm scared him almost made her laugh. Big and bold Dax had a weakness?

"So what do you want from me?" She withheld her sympathy, changing her mind about why he appeared different.

She moved away from the bed.

"You're smart, Katerina. What do you think I want?" He began undressing.

"I wouldn't know." She wanted to avert her eyes but he'd already gone too far in capturing her fascination. A rather charitable amount of him was exposed above the waistband of his trousers. His attractive body begged her to advance.

"No? Well besides finding you an agreeably warm delight as a bed warmer, I find my cabin and my bunk much more homey."

He took one step before the ship pitched to one side and then back again. His footing faltered. However, she was thrown completely off balance and stumbled into him.

She took a quick look out the window, finding the jolt odd. While he held onto her, the ship rocked like a cradle out of control and she read her own thoughts in his eyes.

Katerina couldn't be sure, since she'd never been on the sea, but the sounds, the sudden roughness of the water—she thought volcano.

"Dax?" She moved with him to the bunk and he sat her down.

"That wasn't a storm's doing." He hastily redressed and bundled up in all his outer clothing. "You stay in here."

Stay, her mind grumbled with annoyance.

Dax left her when she wanted to know what went on outside. The ship tilted and cast her to the floor. From there she jerked on her boots. Swiftly, she got up and donned her hooded coat. Dax had a place in her heart that left her little choice than to care for him. She looked in a cabinet for gloves, not for herself as she had hers, but for him since he had left without any. The storm would make the frigid air bitter, the kind of cold not even a polar bear would venture into at night.

With the ship's persistent swaying, each step she took outside the cabin was difficult. She hadn't had much cause to be on a ship, however, she knew this wasn't the way one sailed the Bering Sea.

Katerina heard the shouts from above—angry voices cussing the winds, the waves and God's wrath. The men vented with venomous threats to the heavens and some of the language made her shy away. Determination stiffened her spine and she trudged up the steps.

When the first spray of salty sleet slapped her cheeks and stung her eyes, she let a few of her own curses slip. On the unstable deck she staggered toward the stairs to the quarterdeck where she heard Dax bellowing orders above the storm's din. His voice, a commanding resonance, slashed through the rumble of thunder.

The wide flat rungs were slippery with ice and she tried to make the climb with grace and dignity. Neither were involved when her foot came off the top rung and she fell forward. On the slick surface, gliding like a stunned swan, Katerina crashed into the back of Dax's booted feet.

"I ordered you to stay below." Dax jerked her up from the deck.

Her fear of not knowing what disaster befell them had pushed her to follow him. But it wasn't something she could tell him.

"I don't obey orders, I give them. I wish to know what is going on."

Katerina clutched his arms to keep from ending up flat on the deck.

Dax pointed. "A volcano erupted causing an earthquake."

"Alluvia?"

Her hand shielded her eyes from the icy sleet. She stared at the glow of lava in the darkness. The outline of the mountain, indistinguishable in the night, gave her no clue as to how far they had gone or if her homeland was under attack.

"No." He hugged her. "I don't know what island it is, but I'm sure it's not your home."

He pulled her tighter when the waves rocked them. Katerina opened her coat slightly and took out the gloves.

"You didn't take any when you left." She held them out.

"Thank you." He put them on while never letting her go, and she liked his unyielding embrace.

"Sire." A man worked his way toward them. "Sire, you and the princess should go below."

"Sire?" Katerina screamed over the howling wind.

She pushed away from him, stunned. He grabbed her arm before she got far.

"Just who are you?" she demanded.

Chapter Thirty-three

The ship pitched violently one way and then the other. Dax's hold on Katerina broke. They fell into the rail and with all the horror of a nightmare, he watched the princess topple over the edge.

"Katerina!" He lunged and grasped the fur of her coat.

Her hands went immediately to his forearm. His heart beat like the thunder overhead as he strained to pull her up.

"Hold on."

"Well I'm not letting go!" She clawed at his coat sleeve.

Dark and dangerous, the water below would be the death of her. She'd last no more than a few minutes in the bitter cold. Dax found the heavy coats and gloves made a firm grasp impossible.

"Dax, please don't let me go."

Fear prevented him from answering. In his mind, there was no way he would lose her. He'd thought he had fully resigned himself to the fact that when everything was done, she would go home.

"Dax!"

Looking down into her worried eyes, he knew without a doubt she'd become his future.

"I won't ever let you go," he declared through gritted teeth.

Struggling against the haphazard tilt of the ship, he managed to pull her high enough for her to get a leg over the rail. She hurled herself over the edge and onto him. They fell to the deck.

"See, merely a little effort on your part and we work well together," he teased, hugging her, thankful for his strength and her lightness.

"I thought I was going to die." She sobbed.

He shook his head.

Katerina pressed her mouth to his and he tasted the inexplicable flavor of salty tears, not sea water. Inasmuch as he liked kissing her, in a storm on a wet deck wasn't the time. He pulled her up with him against the bulkhead and together they held the rigging to keep from sliding.

The ship erratically jumped and pitched and waves crashed over the sides, soaking their clothes.

"Sire, the worst is yet to come." A crewman dropped down next to them.

"We're going to die?" Katerina clung to Dax.

"No."

"Yes we are and it's all your fault."

"Junroe, help me get the princess below. The cold is freezing her brain as well as her bottom." He managed his footing and with his man, they got Katerina up.

Across the deck they skated as the ship tipped to accommodate them. Once Dax had her below, he sent Junroe back to his other duties.

"I'm cold and wet." Katerina's teeth chattered.

"And frightened, which is understandable. But if you had stayed in the cabin, you'd be warm and safe. You could have ridden out the upset and then we'd have resumed going to bed." Dax got her in the cabin and pulled off her coat before his own.

"Why does winter have to be so miserably frozen all the time?" She shivered.

"I don't know. So we have more than one reason to get close to a person." He grinned and held her against him.

Her wet gown clung to her. It hugged her as he intended to do as well. She shook violently while he rubbed her icy skin. It worked too quickly and the thaw to her brain came fast.

"He called you sire."

He heard her irritation yet she didn't give up his embrace.

"Yes, well I can't seem to make everyone keep secrets as well as I do." He continued massaging the warmth back into her protesting frame. "It's *King* Daxton James Kent, of Volda."

"King?" She pushed back from him even though her teeth chattered with a harshness that made his jaw ache in sympathy. "You lied about who you were, but why?"

"I had my reasons and they're not important." He pulled a blanket off the bunk and held it up. "Take off the gown."

"I will not." She folded her arms.

"I'll do it for you."

The idea of stripping the clothes from her did more to warm him than a fire ever could. He really hoped she'd refuse because he liked wrestling with her. Not that fighting a woman gave him a thrill. Katerina made things a bit more interesting. Each time he won, she had the control of when. She surrendered only when she had put up enough struggle to keep her dignity. He found no fault with her being proud.

"Well, don't look." She dropped her arms.

"I've seen most of you, beautiful."

"Just shut your eyes...please."

Dax closed his eyes and held the blanket higher. "You've got two minutes."

"But what do I put on?"

He heard the lid to his trunk open.

"Is this all right?"

Dax opened his eyes and lowered the blanket to see one of his shirts dangling from the hook of her finger. "Yes, Princess. You've my permission to wear any of my clothes...sixty seconds left, Katerina."

"Don't you dare peek." She turned her back to him and hurried to pull off the gown.

Dax cracked one eye open and dared a glance. The very exquisite and Katerina stood naked. He held his breath lest she'd know he observed.

Covered in goose flesh, her pink bottom was a marvelous sight. The curves made his fingers itch to touch her. He barely got a look at her back before she dropped the shirt over her head. She went to the trunk for more clothes.

"Can I lower my hands now?"

"I don't see why not. They're not doing much good since you cheated."

"I—"

"Don't lie. I know you peeked." She put on a wool jacket and climbed on the bed to wrap her legs in the blanket.

"How'd you know?"

"You stopped breathing." Her fingers waved at him. "Now you, take off those clothes before you catch your death."

"You care?"

"Only as far as you getting me back to my kingdom." She worked at adjusting the blanket and the jacket. "Can't you make this cabin warmer?"

Dax peeled away his wet clothes one at a time.

"Aren't you going to ask me to close my eyes?" Her eyes widened as his shirt disappeared and then his boots.

"Watch and enjoy all you want, my princess."

He laughed when he dropped his trousers and her hands flew up over her eyes.

"Hurry up," she insisted.

With each stitch of clothing he removed, her fingers less completely covered her eyes.

He didn't tell her he was dressed. She knew and lowered her hands.

"Where are you going?" She grabbed the headboard as the ship pitched hard to one side and then the other.

Dax put on several layers of clothes and as he buttoned his coat, he smiled. "I have a ship to see about. The captain is a good seaman, but I need to know what is going on in case a decision has to be made."

"A decision?" She slid off the bunk clutching the blanket around her.

"Get back in the bed." He ushered her to the mattress. "I'll make sure everything is all right."

"Dax?" She gripped his sleeve and held him.

The worry in her eyes mesmerized him. In all his travels, he'd never seen anyone other than his sister look drained by fear.

"I'll be back. You haven't any need to worry about me." He lifted her chin and captured her parted lips.

He withdrew his mouth slowly, but she leaned, following with her puckered lips. His arms bound her to him and he plunged into a deep kiss until she breathlessly pushed at him. Her futile efforts subsided when he didn't let go.

"I'm not worried about your return," she grumbled.

"No?" He kissed her again and her mouth followed his every move.

"No," she reaffirmed when he stopped his exhausting pursuit of her tongue.

"If I should fall overboard, you'd not miss me?" He teased her unmercifully and each time he did, her lovely face pinched with dreadful wrinkles.

"Dax, please."

"I'll be all right." He cupped the side of her face.

"Just be careful. I need you...I mean I need this ship to get me home."

He smiled and kissed her again with tenderness for her confession. While she tried to adjust her words to sound selfish, the attempt had failed. Her soft lips attached to his and he found her doing all the kissing. He knew he shouldn't have chuckled, except her cute front of resistance had an adorable appeal.

"I really don't care about you," she reiterated.

"I know," he whispered and pulled her up from the bed.

Her arms folded around him. He didn't want to leave. Her brown watery eyes stared at him with uncertainty. It made him feel unscrupulously low.

"I've got to go." He moved her to a sitting position on the side of the bed. "We'll resume this when I get back."

His heart gave a rough thump to his chest when she nodded mutely as he left the cabin. He liked spontaneity, he reveled in adventure and he loved that he had met a woman who immersed herself in the same.

"Sire, the volcano has triggered another." Junroe met him in the passageway.

"Is it Volda or Alluvia?"

"No sire, an island to the west."

"I'll be up shortly. See that everything is battened down for the tremors. It won't take long to toss us about some more."

"And if a tsunami should rise up?"

"What do you want me to say, Junroe? We've no control over such things, but I expect you to protect the princess."

"Which princess, sire?"

Dax turned to look at his cabin and that of his sister's. If something disastrous happened, who would he go to first? How could he tell Junroe to help Giselle and not Katerina?

"We'll not have to decide which because we'll not have that decision come to us today," he said, unable to make a choice.

He went to Giselle's cabin and knocked sharply.

"Come in," she answered in a sob.

"What is this?" Upon seeing tears, he rushed to the bed and hugged her. "Everything will be all right."

"He hates me." She wept into his fur collar.

"I told you not to get emotionally involved." He kissed her forehead. "It was inevitable that he'd not be happy with our plan."

"And you have no feelings for the princess?"

"How could I?" He hugged her tighter trying to dispel the guilt of his lie and his other thoughts. "She is a means to an end. Besides I've not known her long enough to have anything more than a mild interest in the haughty woman. She's mean, bossy and most definitely childish. I don't think she cares a scrap about anyone other than herself."

"And it might be better that I don't." Katerina's voice flew at him from the open doorway.

"What are you doing here?" Dax got up from the bunk and pulled her in the room. "You were to stay safely in my cabin."

"I came because I thought your sister might be frightened and I...I stupidly thought I could be of comfort in your absence." She pulled her arm from his grip. "It was foolish of me, I know. It must be another bad trait in my bloodline. I'll try not to indulge my immaturity again by thinking I'm of use to anybody."

She swiftly left the cabin and he looked on, stunned. He shouldn't have been, since their last kiss gave him insight into where her affections lay.

"Dax, you've hurt her." Giselle pushed him toward the door. "Go after her and tell her you didn't mean it."

"Why?"

"Because you don't. As much as I love you for trying to talk me out of my own misery by saying you feel nothing for her, it's obvious she's found a place in your heart."

"I don't know about that. I've got to go up on deck and Katerina's ego can wait until I have time for mending fences."

"Dax, just stop for a few seconds and tell her you didn't mean it the way it sounded," Giselle pleaded. "If she's angry with you, she'll be angry with me."

"No. Now, stay in this cabin and I'll be around in several hours to check on you." He cupped her chin. "She's upset but she won't be angry with you."

He left the cabin and stopping in front of his, he put his hand out for the door handle. It flew open without his help and he stepped back as Katerina swept out of the cabin.

"I'm sorry," she said. "I was still disturbed by my near drowning and I now realize ours is a pretend affair and feelings have no bearing on the matter. I'm going to sit with your sister whether you think I care or not."

Dax bowed his head and let her go. She faltered with the sway of the vessel and his foot moved toward her. He stretched to grab her and stopped.

She held a hand to the wall and looked back. "I'm fine. You can go now," she said in her most royally commanding tone.

"Yes, Your Highness." He bowed his head and turned on his heel.

Katerina had him running from a confusion he hadn't quite figured out how to handle.

Chapter Thirty-four

Katerina huffed at Dax's attitude and waltzed down the passage to Giselle's door. She tapped once and the door opened.

"I'd say I'd like to keep you company, but actually I'm nervous and felt it might be good for the both of us." Katerina entered only after Giselle nodded in agreement.

"I'd like that very much, Your Highness." Giselle moved clothes from a chair. "Please have a seat."

"Thank you, Princess." Katerina sat.

"So, my brother has told you who he is."

"Yes, and I dare say it wasn't his plan." She lifted a book on the table. "Has he been king long?"

"Nine years. When our parents died Dax had to run a country and raise me."

"I'm sorry. It must have been hard for you as well. My mother died when I was a little younger then you are now. How old were you?"

"I was seven and while I remember them, Dax always took care of me, so he's been both brother and father to me." She twisted her hands together. "He's a very caring man and he didn't mean what he said about you earlier. He's just had much to deal with in the past couple years I think he's afraid to involve himself with anyone on a personal level."

Katerina thought of the deal she had with Dax.

"What he said was to make you feel better. Dax and I get along extremely well." Katerina smiled.

"But he—"

"He likes to act as if our relationship is not important because it would be inappropriate for two rulers to display open affection when they are going to be...well...Giselle, whatever Dax and I seem like on the outside is nothing like what we might feel on the inside. I like him as much as you like my brother. Only sometimes things get in the way of us... Oh, let's talk of something else."

The sudden pitch of the ship halted their bonding and Katerina fell on the floor. Giselle crashed into a cabinet. Her squeal came painfully shrill and Katerina crawled toward her as the blood trickled down the girl's face.

"Hold still," Katerina grabbed what might have been a shirt and dabbed at Giselle's forehead.

"Ouch. Oh, it hurts," she cried.

"It's not bad." Katerina patted it again.

"Will it leave a scar? I don't want to have a horrible scar."

Katerina smiled and rubbed the back of her finger on Giselle's cheek. "No man would ever care about one little nick such as this, even if it does leave a mark."

The ship rolled again and Katerina pulled Giselle into a niche between bunk and cabinet to prevent them from tumbling around the floor. When the door flew open she expected Dax, not Balthazar.

"Kat, are you all right?" He knelt before them.

She nodded and smiled. His gaze never left Giselle's and she forgave his concern wandering to another woman.

"Would you help Giselle to the bunk and I'll get some water to clean her cut."

Balthazar did not hesitate. His hand went under Giselle's arms and he pulled her to her feet. His arm surrounded her waist to guide her to the bunk. Katerina managed to get to her feet just as Dax entered the cabin. The ship continued to rock and he grabbed her.

"Giselle?" He looked beyond her to his sister.

"It's a little cut." Katerina's hand thumped his hard chest gently. "She'll be fine."

"And you?" He lifted her chin.

"A bruise or two, nothing more." She moved out of his arms and poured water from a jug into a small bowl. "What is going on out there?" she whispered, as he held her hips to keep her steady.

"Aftershocks, I reckon."

They both turned their heads to look at Giselle. Her giggle sounded misplaced given the gravity of their situation.

"Your scar would be a distinguishing mark of bravery, Your Highness. Mine would be of clumsiness," Giselle told Balthazar.

☙ ❧

Dax strolled along the balcony of his palace and watched his sister sit in the gazebo. When recalling the final hours of their voyage, he worried over the sudden change in Balthazar's mood. He spent every possible minute with Giselle. It seemed hard to believe that once Katerina informed Balthazar she would marry the man who kidnapped them, the prince would take the news graciously.

Giselle's return to happiness with the attentive prince looked all too possible a calamity in the making. Dax hated to involve her in the bitter games of rulers. She should have had a simple, happy life, instead of the hurtful one she endured.

When Prince Balthazar joined her, Dax waited for a new upheaval. In a way he couldn't blame the man for feeling betrayed. However, with nobility they all had a burden to bear. If he had any intelligence, the prince would see Giselle was in love with him and he'd return the sentiment willingly.

Dax turned at the sound of the door and saw Katerina. She had left her hair loose and it cascaded over her thick wool cloak.

"She's in love with him," she commented.

"Infatuation is hardly love." He walked away.

Things were still wrong with his plan. His emotions only worsened his problems. He looked back from the palace doors. Katerina had slipped into a place in his heart he couldn't close off. As she watched her brother and his sister, he wondered if she felt as jealous as he did. Balthazar and Giselle had nothing to stop them from falling in love. The weight of duty didn't keep them from expressing their feelings.

When Katerina's gaze turned to him, he fled the sadness he saw in her face. No woman should ever be unhappy and he didn't know how to change her expression quite yet.

Dax went to his study to handle affairs of the kingdom. He shoved Katerina as far from his thoughts as he could. It seemed near impossible to set her aside since she make a large impact on his life.

"Sire?" A servant entered.

Dax looked up. He set his seal inside the casket and closed the lid. "Yes?"

The servant bowed, stepped forward with hesitation and folded his hands together over the work apron he wore. “Sire, you said we were to tell you of Princess Katerina or Prince Balthazar’s movements, if they did something unusual.”

“Yes.” Dax stood with immediate concern.

“The princess has left the palace by way of the underground catacombs. Stefan followed her. He thinks she is in search of the hot pool.”

“Stefan?” Dax moved out from behind his desk. “Stefan, from Alluvia?”

“Yes, I do believe he is from Alluvia, sire.”

“Why did he follow her?”

“Your orders, sire. You instructed everyone to keep a close watch on the prince and princess and make sure they were protected. While the catacombs are usually safe, she could get lost.”

Dax couldn’t control the speed with which his heart pounded. Somehow, Stefan had slipped his mind. He had meant to send the man back to Alluvia upon his arrival. It exceeded coincidence that the Stefan Katerina called out for in her sexual rapture was the same.

“Should I send others to bring her back?” the servant asked.

“I’ll take care of this myself.”

Dax ran through the palace to the entrance of the catacombs. He bumped into everything, leaving a wake of broken vases on the floor. It seemed, even in the wide halls, tables were in the way of reaching Katerina. He didn’t know what he planned to do if he found her in a compromising position with Stefan, because he didn’t know what to do about any of his feelings.

The passageways to the catacombs were as intricate as the tunnels beneath the mountain. A person could be lost for a long time if they didn't know which routes to follow. He headed straight for the pool of fresh volcanically heated water.

The closer he got, the harder he found it to breath.

The rarity of her voice, exquisite in song, echoed through the cave to wrap around his heart. He froze in his tracks, afraid to find her happiness came from a man who had first introduced her to sexual pleasures.

He didn't remember how long he stood, listening to her sing, waiting to hear a conversation that might kill him. When none came, he threw back his shoulders to confront the discreet lovers.

His eyes scanned the area of the cavern. Katerina swam in the crystal waters lit by a natural opening in the mountain. Sunlight streamed in. Her bare skin glistened as if she were bathed in diamond dust.

"Where's Stefan?"

She twirled around and blinked water from her eyes.

"I was wondering how long it would take you to come after your servant told you I came down here."

"Where is he?"

"Who?"

"You know who."

"You should have told me Stefan was here." She splashed water over her shoulders. "I wouldn't have been so embarrassed running into him in the palace."

"So, where is he? Hiding?"

She smiled with a wicked delight that sparkled in her eyes. She knew it would torment him to know of her liaison with a servant in his palace.

"He's not here," she finally replied.

"You shouldn't be here alone. Get out."

"I will not."

He took off his jacket and laid it over a rock near her clothes.

"What are you doing?"

"Coming to get you out."

He shed his clothes slowly, with purpose. Either Katerina would be outraged, indifferent or eager for him to join her. What game she played today intrigued him.

"Why is Stefan not here?" he asked.

"I sent him home to Alluvia. I told him of my father's death so he could return."

"You don't wish him to be here, with you?"

"No, I have no wish to know Stefan in the way you think. To keep him around would be to his disadvantage. It would be sad to think he'd pine for me when I am unattainable."

Dax held her gaze. He never hoped to see a woman as structurally exquisite as she and he'd never find one as utterly charming that he'd do her bidding.

"Why have you never married?" she asked.

"Never wanted a wife."

"What about an heir?"

"I said I never wanted a wife. However when the time is right, I'll have one for that purpose."

"I agree with that philosophy. Why should a person be obligated to one when she has not met all possibilities?"

Dax waded in until he was waist deep. The water was the perfect temperature. He moved steadily to Katerina and when he was in front of her, he bent down.

"I should not like anyone looking upon you this way and I forgive your impetuousness." He straightened without touching a kiss to her inviting lips.

"You forgive." Without thought to her nudity, Katerina lunged at him.

Unprepared and losing his footing, he fell back under the water. His reflexes were good and he caught her wrist, taking her with him. Surfacing, he dragged her closer. She coughed with a gurgle that wracked her body and he held her sleek frame against him.

"You could have drowned me," she gasped and coughed again with her face pressed to his chest.

Their naked bodies melded together and she tensed when she realized that fact.

"Do I let go, Princess?"

Her heart beat thunderously with his, her chest heaved with her breathless pants. If she said yes, would he let her go? She had put them in a very precarious situation.

She shook her head and tilted it back to catch his mouth coming down on hers. She curled her fingers into his hair and held his head, not letting him stop. This time there would be no interruptions and no withdrawal for any reason.

Dax took in every contour of Katerina's mouth—her slick teeth, the corrugations on the roof of her mouth and the smoothness of her tongue. He drove to a deeper exploration. The orifice, likened to her cunt, had a hidden quality he desired to experience again. The way he could fuck her throat and have the muscles constrict heightened his orgasm. Yet, as much as he wanted to feel the suckling of her lips over his swelling erection, he wanted to plant himself deep into her guarded sex more.

"Oh Dax, I only told the servant to say I was with Stefan so you would come here."

"You needn't use a ploy to get my attention." He kissed her harder. "Just ask me for what you want."

"I want you," she sighed in surrender.

Chapter Thirty-five

Katerina didn't want her first time with Dax to be in a cave. She wanted the softness of a bed and the hardness of him pressing her into the mattress. He must have read her thoughts when he led her to her clothes.

She didn't say anything as he dressed. She feared one word would spiral her hopes out of control. So many times they had come close and parted on raw nerves. Circumstances had not changed.

She took his hand when he held it out. "You're not going to change your mind, are you? About wanting me?"

"No."

"I mean, now that you know about Stefan and me."

He stopped and looked her. "I don't know if that's what angered me the most. You called out his name when I—"

"Dax I...when he said it was his mother's house you stayed at, I thought he told you about us."

"You tell me now."

She bit her trembling lip to still it.

"Well?"

"It meant nothing."

"I'm sure it meant a great deal."

Every time she though of Dax with another woman, jealousy stirred in her. His expression held something similar and she had no wish to discuss intimacies from her past with the man she wanted in her future. The small time period when a boy awakened her sexual curiosities was a fading memory—a part of her life she no longer needed to rely on for comfort.

Tears formed and rolled down her cheeks as she worried Dax would never forget another man had once touched her intimately.

Dax pulled her to him. “Don’t cry.”

“This changes everything between us.”

“Not if you don’t feel anything for him.” He held her at arm’s length. “Do you?”

She shook her head. “Not for many years.”

“Even seeing him didn’t stir old desires?”

“Not even a sliver of one.” She hugged him when he let her move back into his arms. “I want you, Dax.”

He pulled her head away and gazed lovingly into her eyes. “And I want you, Katerina.”

Her name on his lips fascinated her. Dax put his mouth against hers and his kiss lingered. Then he began a hot pursuit down her neck. His passion made her weak in the knees and she hung onto him as he lifted her off the ground.

“Where are we going?” She nuzzled her face alongside his.

“Somewhere clean, soft and comfortable. Is that agreeable?”

“Mmmm, very.”

Dax carried her through the maze of tunnels. With the lighting too dim to make out his features, Katerina slid her fingers over his face. She stroked from his brow to his jaw, finding the textures to her liking.

He stopped before they reached the hidden door back into the palace and stood her on the ground.

"This doesn't look like anything you described." Her laugh was short as he pushed her against a wall of stone.

His hot breath rushed into her mouth and, for several minutes, she reveled in his adoring hold.

"It's an interlude." He answered once his deep, soul-reaching kiss ended.

"Let's not have many more. I'm wet and cold."

"As you wish." He slid an arm under her legs and swung her back up, cradling her to his chest.

"I do, right now."

To her bedchamber they went. She didn't give a second thought to the servants who watched. Nor did she care if her brother and Giselle witnessed Dax take her to bed as a lover.

The door of her room thumped the wall when he kicked it open. It slammed shut as his boot gave it a quick nudge.

"I could have walked. You didn't wear yourself out, did you?"

"I have hardly used an ounce of energy carrying you." He sat her on the bed.

"I should get a towel and dry my hair."

She watched Dax walk to a cabinet and come back with a large white towel. He sat behind her and rubbed it over her hair.

"If I don't comb it, it'll turn into a horribly tangled mess like on the ship."

Dax kissed her shoulder. "Nervous?"

She nodded.

"Why?"

"You might change your mind." She looked over her shoulder.

He held her jaw and kissed her cheek. His lips warmly assured her he wouldn't change his mind.

He tossed the towel away. Taking her hand, he pulled her up. Just as he dressed her in the cavern, he undressed her. His kisses burned a blazing trail downward. The pause he took at her breasts and belly made her shiver.

She watched him fling her clothes away after she stepped out of them.

"I like you naked." He rose up and stepped back. "I like the pink shade of your creamy skin."

She wanted to fold her arms up and hide what he stared at, but she couldn't deny she loved the way his approving eyes scorched her insides.

"You want me to close my eyes?"

She shook her head. "Will you undress now?"

"You think I should?"

She couldn't help smiling and nodded again.

He peeled every piece of wet clothing from his muscled body. She had seen bits and pieces of him before. A complete view would be a heavenly sight and she swallowed with anticipation. In the cavern, he had stripped down, but she hadn't the luxury of brighter lighting.

His shirt landed on the floor. His trousers dropped to the tops of his boots. He sat on the chair and tugged the brown leather knee boots off. The trousers went by the wayside.

"I'll get in the bed." Her cheeks heated and she turned away.

She hardly had a knee on the mattress, when Dax's large hands grabbed her hips. He flung her over on her back.

"Hey beautiful, your backside is as gorgeous as the front."

She lifted her eyes slowly, taking in every inch of his lean, hard body. Muscles rippled everywhere.

"Dax, would you make love to me without the preliminaries?"

"Without?" He put a knee between hers.

"You've started many times before and I...I want you in me. I want your cock buried in me so I'll not wonder any longer."

Dax, being Dax, took his time. She felt anxious, knowing something would happen to stop him. When a tap came to her door, a nervous whimper brought him down onto her.

"Ignore it." He kissed her.

She rubbed her hands over his chest as he moved to fit his cock inside her.

The knock grew louder.

"Yes?" she answered.

Dax kissed her neck.

"Kat, I have something important to talk to you about," Balthazar announced.

"Not now." She slid her hands over Dax's back.

"Kat, I need to speak to you, now."

"I'm busy." She bit her lip as Dax pushed into her.

He fit tight at the entrance. Her eyes never left his.

"Kat!" Balthazar yelled.

"Persistent, isn't he?" Dax pressed his mouth to hers and flexed his hips.

She felt a burning sting and her cry remained contained. His mouth moved with gentle brushes over her lips as he drew back.

"Are you all right?" he whispered.

"Yes."

Dax started to move with an easy rock against her. She put a hand to his face and stroked his cheek.

"Come on, Kat, this will only take a minute," Balthazar insisted.

"We'll be a little longer than a minute," Dax shouted.

"Oh Dax," she groaned.

"Nothing is going to stop me from making love to you this time, Princess. Not even your brother's ill timing."

His mouth crashed against hers and his tongue probed inside. Waves of breathless pleasure twisted her insides. She lifted to his plunges and the tension escalated. Her whines mixed a duet of sounds with his grunts and groans. She felt him holding back and she impulsively dug her nails into the cheeks of his ass. It brought him down harder on her.

"Easy, Katerina, I'll give you what you want."

He pushed faster into her and, in one glorious heat of the moment, she froze. Her body jolted uncontrollably.

Dax held onto her, but it wasn't enough. His strangled groan vibrated against the side of her head.

She didn't know how long they clung together. Their wet, perspiring flesh molded into one form. She cried for the joy she felt and she hugged him tight.

"You're crying again."

She splashed kisses on his bristled jaw. "Yes."

"Do you want me off?"

"No." She tightened her hold on him.

Eventually, Dax shifted his weight to the mattress and held her against his side. Mindlessly, his hand swept over her hot, damp skin as they talked. The inconsequential topics were a form of getting to know one another better. Childhoods, fond memories of parents and even secret dreams were shared. As he opened up to her, she felt as if she had found a soul mate.

When Dax told her every detail about her uncle's plans he left nothing out. She accepted his apology wholeheartedly, knowing the predicament her uncle had put him in left him no choice other than go along with the scheme to prevent her or Balthazar from marrying.

After hours of comforting relaxation, Katerina pushed her fingers down Dax's abdomen and fondled the dark, wiry hair around the base of his cock. She wanted to have him in her again and she made it known.

"Temptress," he moaned.

"I've got years to make up for." She slid a leg over him and straddled his thighs.

"What are you up to?"

"I think it's you that's up." She gave his cock a teasing swirl of her finger around the rim.

She scooted closer, letting his erection rise against her belly.

"Not fully, but I'm getting there in a damn hurry." He pulled his cock out of the way and rubbed his fingers into her soft, wet flesh. "This will help."

"Me or you?" She giggled.

His fingers slipped inside her and drew the wetness up over her clit. A shudder rippled through her body. He teased and pleased her until she was mad with desire.

"Dax." She leaned forward and put her hands on his chest.

"Wait." He thrust his fingers in her and pumped them, nudging her clit with his knuckles.

She couldn't wait. Her insides exploded almost immediately. She sat up and while rocking back and forth, she gripped his hard shaft, pulling and pushing the thin, delicate skin up and down. Lifting on her knees, using his chest as support, she eased down onto his throbbing cock.

"You feel amazing," he groaned as she took him deep into her moist heat, as far her body would let him go.

"You're pretty magnificent yourself."

Dax grabbed her hips and took control of her rhythm. She liked the way he showed her without making her feel silly or stupid for not knowing what to do when they had sex. He let her test and explore, but mostly, he allowed her to question without fear he'd laugh.

"Do you like me on top?"

"For a while, sweetness." His fingers dug into her waist and he thrust with a bruising fierceness.

She tossed her head back in glorious abandon. Her orgasm shook her and Dax rubbed at her sides. His hands cupped her breasts, squeezing and massaging them until her tense body started to relax.

It was over and she felt a slight disappointment he hadn't reached the point she had. Her insides twitched and held him, and suddenly Dax's grip went to her upper arms. He flipped her on her back, rolling with her, and in several thrusts, he released an imposing roar.

Her body responded to the liquid heat and she climaxed in a nerve-tingling orgasm.

"Dax." She pressed kisses to his taut lips and clenched jaw.

Tears rolled from the outside corners of her eyes and slid across her temples to her hair. Dax kissed away the wetness first and then their lips clung together.

For several minutes they remained together panting, recovering from the sweet agony of sexual emotions.

"Katerina, I have a plan that might save your lands and mine. It really is our last chance."

He rolled off her and stared at the ceiling. The golden fretwork laced the room in light and shadows. Their lovemaking left him sated and yet eager for their next coupling.

"I don't want to think of that now." She rolled to her side and pressed the length of her slender silky body to him. "I finally get you in my bed and now you want to spoil it with a problem there is no getting out of."

"You're a very selfish woman at times."

"I'm sure you'll put me in my place as you've done since we met." She smiled. "What is your plan?"

"I think there's a way to get what we both want and need." He slid a hand up under her breast. He let his thumb brush over the tip to tease her nipple into that submissive hard pearl he loved to suck.

Katerina glided up his chest, her intent visible. He looked at her wet, kiss-swollen lips and wanted them to torture him again.

"I've surrendered, King Daxton."

He fanned his hands across her buttocks.

"Oh, and you don't think I've noticed?" He massaged the supple cheeks and manipulated her hips, wedging his cock against the splendor of her wet cunt.

"I meant for real. I could surrender Alluvia to you."

"My plan, remember?" He kissed her, never thinking he could love a woman more than he did right then. "I'll be the one doing the surrendering. I figure if you make Volda a realm of your kingdom, then Lord Talbot wouldn't dare attack. With your army ready to defend Alluvian lands, he'd not destroy Volda."

"You can't just give me your kingdom and think it will make things all right. Besides, if Volda belonged to Alluvia, he'd still gain control over it when I lose my kingdom."

"You don't understand. I surrender Volda to *you*, Princess Katerina. Your signature and mine on a paper would give you my lands to take as your own, and to save Alluvia, I marry you."

"That is not why I let you make love to me. I don't wish to govern your land or you." She lifted a robe and slipped it on to cover up all he loved to look at.

"This way you rule Alluvia and Volda." Dax picked up his trousers and slid them on. "I'm willing to sacrifice my crown for peace. What about you? Would it be so bad to have me as your consort?"

When she turned, she didn't give him any indication of her thoughts.

"I'll only accept Volda as a union, not a conquered land." She went to the writing desk and picked up a sheet of parchment.

"A union, how?"

He watched her lift the pen from its holder. She wrote as she spoke.

"I decree that by my power as regent of Alluvia, I take in the boundaries of Volda to be a part of my kingdom by wish and by grant of King Daxton. As in my power as acting sovereign, I thus give my hand to King Daxton that our union of body is equal under the eyes of God and in the laws of matrimony." She dipped the pen in the inkwell and handed it to him. "By signing this, you contract to be my king as well as my husband."

Dax took the pen without hesitation and scribed his name, making every swirl cross through one of hers until the last loop circled their names.

"I'll not add it to this decree, but I hope as your king and husband, you'll also find it a bonus to have me as a friend and lover."

Her eyes watered and the nod of her head was all he needed.

"A ceremony, short, private and immediate would end your problems. Then I can deal with Lord Talbot." He held his hands out to her.

"We will deal with my uncle together."

Dax pulled her close and kissed the top of her head as she laid it on his chest. They would be good together, he thought. There was nothing but a bright future for him as long as she was willing to be this generous with her heart.

Epilogue

The ballroom calmed to a faint hum of whispering. Rumors had circulated, but no one knew for sure why King Daxton called for a celebration. Nevertheless, hundreds of guests stood anxious to hear the important announcement.

Katerina sat in the small chamber with Giselle. She went periodically to the heavy drapes and peered out at the simplicity of the room lit brightly with whale oil lanterns.

"Your Majesty, you really should sit and relax," Giselle suggested. "There is nothing to be nervous about. Dax and Balthazar have everything under control."

Giselle sat as pretty as a doll on the edge of the settee. Her hands clasped in her lap remained still, her tone unwavering. Then why would she be on edge. These were her people, her home and she already had their respect.

"I'm calmer when I keep moving." Katerina let go of the curtain and shuffled across the polished stone floor.

"Your Majesty, maybe if you—"

"Please," Katerina snapped. "Please, Giselle," she said softly. "I do wish you would call me Katerina. It makes me uncomfortable to hear you humble yourself. It could as easily have been you as queen to my brother."

"I'm terribly sorry. I've sort of gotten used to it and you're...well you're more befitting the title than anyone I have ever met. I thought it would be an insult to call you by your given name." She looked down at her feet sliding back and forth on the floor. Her hands smoothed and wrinkled her dress.

"Say my name," Katerina commanded.

"Katerina."

"See, you say it with such elegance it makes me hear your respect. I command you, Princess Giselle of Volda, to always call me by my given name. Except of course when not prudent to do so, like in front of commoners and such, but I think you know what I mean."

"Yes, I understand." Giselle smiled.

"We will be the best of friends and the closest of any sisters. Your wedding to Balthazar will be the grandest that anyone has ever seen."

"I'm frightened, Katerina. What if something goes wrong? What if—"

"No what ifs. There's not a place for them in this world right now."

A door opened and Dax came in with his usual brusque and hurried manner. His black hair, twisted on all the ends, suggested he'd been outside. His reddened cheeks were a second giveaway.

"Look at you. What a mess your hair is." Giselle immediately went to comb her fingers through his locks. Then she stepped back. "Forgive me." She looked at Katerina. "I've always fussed over him and his appearance. I'll have to learn it is no longer my place."

"Who said it wasn't your place, Giselle." Katerina put a hand to her back. "You'll always be his sister and besides, he likes the attention."

Dax took Katerina's hand and bowed down to kiss her knuckles. "Are you ready?"

"No." She shook her head nervously. They were about to boldly make a move on two lands and set down in history a very vivid mark no one would likely forget.

Dax led her out the door, along the hall and down the stone steps.

"Ladies and Gentlemen, Their Royal Majesties, King Daxton and his wife, Queen Katerina of Alluvia."

Katerina smiled and looked at Dax. The cheers and clapping was enormous. Her heart fluttered with the acceptance. The crowd was overwhelming, with people of many different stations. Dax had not yet made his announcement and she scanned the room for her Uncle Talbot.

It wasn't hard to find him. His face displayed anger well and his next moves worried her. His steps were quick and he aimed for the dais she stood on with Dax. The guards stopped him.

"Dax?" she whispered, concerned Talbot would do something drastically stupid.

"Let him stew." He raised his hands to silence the crowd. "I have some wonderful news for my people of Volda!"

Talbot pushed past the guards and came at Katerina. "Your marriage means nothing in Alluvia."

Katerina held her head high and looked down her nose at her uncle. "I am in Alluvia, dear uncle."

"People of Volda." Dax shouted. "By my decree and marriage to Queen Katerina, we have joined our lands and are now one kingdom united! May our prosperity and futures look brighter than they ever have!"

Over the loud cheers and commotion, Lord Talbot growled. "You cannot get away with this, Katerina. And you, King Daxton, you will regret the day you thought to double-cross me."

"The only regret I have is trying to destroy another kingdom to save my own. However, I did remedy that. As well as find a queen to cherish." Dax picked up Katerina's hand and kissed her gloved fingers.

Talbot spun on his hard-heeled boots and, at Dax's slight nod, the guards grabbed him.

"What is the meaning of this?" Talbot demanded.

"You are being arrested as a traitor to the crown of Alluvia," Katerina informed him, holding back her satisfied smile.

"You have no proof."

"Oh, but you're wrong." Balthazar marched across the stone floor with two guards at his side, each holding a soldier. "These are your men, are they not?"

Lord Talbot said nothing.

"They were ready for us, Lord Talbot," the soldier blurted out.

"You!" Dax pointed at the prisoners. "You are the one who pretended to be a guard at the palace and tried assassinating the prince on the cliffs."

Alarmed by the memory, Katerina hugged Dax's arm.

"Have mercy, Your Majesty. Lord Talbot ordered..."

"Shut up you fool." Talbot glared at him.

"As Volda is now part of Alluvia, we all have rights here." Balthazar smirked.

"And you foolish boy, you have given up the crown to a woman?" Talbot asked.

"My sister has my blessings. She will rule jointly and proficiently with her king. I, on the other hand…" He looked around and from the side of the dais saw Giselle. His hand stretched out to her and she flew across the floor to him. "I'll have a quiet, happy life with my future bride, Princess Giselle."

Katerina smiled. Nothing could be more promising than all their happiness.

"Take Lord Talbot to the prison," Dax ordered. "Everyone, let us continue our celebration."

"Everything went well?" Katerina asked Balthazar.

"Very smoothly. I explained we already had Talbot in custody and that if they gave up without a fight, we could all go home happy and alive. Seems Talbot's army was not as willing to lay down their lives as he thought they were." Balthazar pulled Giselle tight. "Now if Your Royal Majesties would excuse us, I owe this lady a dance." He bowed and Giselle curtseyed.

"Yes, be off with you." Dax waved a hand at them and then took Katerina's arm. "Shall we sit, my queen?"

She took her turn slow, graceful and with a regal air she never felt more fully than right then. She hadn't noticed the throne chairs before, but they were identical, except one was slightly worn.

"You'll have to break in your own chair," he whispered. "But I assure you, it's quite comfortable."

She let out a small giggle and sat. Dax leaned down. "I'm sure this breaks some protocol." He put his hands on the arms of the chairs and kissed her deeply, then withdrew. "I know I have shown you how I feel, but I have been remiss not telling you explicitly and emphatically."

Katerina blinked and still she couldn't hold back joyful tears.

"I love you," he said loud enough for anyone standing within ten feet to hear. "And I promise to tell you that every chance I get for the rest of my life."

Katerina wrapped her arms around his neck and kissed him hard as he pulled her to her feet. "I don't care what rules we're breaking. We'll make new ones." She kissed him again.

"I do think you have a splendid idea there, my queen. Maybe instead of sitting here like statues for the public to see, you'd like to dance and mingle with our subjects?"

"It would be my honor." She took his arm and let him lead her down near her brother and his sister. "I love you, Dax. I can't tell you when I realized it, but that night you said you didn't want to be my suitor, something started to die in me. I understand now, it was my hope of being loved."

"I know exactly when you had my heart." He brushed back a lock of sable.

"When?"

"The night I left you in the throne room I forgot to ask you something. I stuck my head in the door, and sweetheart, you can't imagine how much it pained me to see I'd reduced you to tears." He kissed her lightly.

"Tell me again that you love me."

"Now how honest can an answer be if the queen is requesting one?" He smiled. "I love everything about you, Katerina."

"I love you too, from the very bottom of my soul."

Dax twirled her around into his arms. "Now that we've got that settled. How about we discuss producing an heir to our dynasty?"

"Discuss?" She raised her eyebrow. "I much prefer action."

"Balthazar?" Dax elbowed him. "We're going to slip out for a while, make whatever excuses you want."

"Dax!" Katerina squealed as he snatched her hand and towed her across the room. "I didn't mean now."

"No?" He stopped and looked back at her. "Remember we can change the rules."

"I don't know." She hesitated.

"Are you worried how it will look for the king and queen to disappear from a royal function?"

"I don't know. I've never given it much thought."

He gave her that intense look filled with the memories of everything they had shared in each other's arms. How could she resist?

"Oh, who cares." She laughed and pushed him to take her to a quiet place where they could reaffirm their love.

Dax spun her to stand behind the curtains, concealing them from everyone in the room. She smiled, wanting nothing more than to be forever in his arms.

"I love you." She puckered for his kiss.

"Katerina, my life began when you came into it."

"I know. Now kiss me." She grabbed his jacket and pulled him to her. "Just please, kiss me."

About the Author

To learn more about Brenda Williamson, please visit her at www.BrendaWilliamson.com. You can also send an email to Brenda at Brenda@BrendaWilliamson.com.

To keep updated on her upcoming releases, join Brenda's newsletter - http://www.BrendaWilliamson.com/Newsletter.htm. You can also hang out and talk to Brenda, along with other readers and writers at http://www.groups.yahoo.com/group/BrendaWilliamsonRomanceParty/

Look for these titles

Now Available:

A Desperate Longing
Devil's Kiss
One Bashful Lady
Sword of Rhoswen
Wolverton Blood

What do you get when you put a lustful, silver-tongued devil in the path of a hard-hearted woman fighting love? Sparks and something even hotter...

Devil's Kiss

© 2006 Brenda Williamson

U.S. Marshal Jack McCay tracks outlaws for a profession and sweet-talks women out of their clothes for pleasure. When he begins to hunt a vicious killer, he meets one beautiful woman resistant to his charm.

Tessa Jane Creager searches for her family's murderer. The wanted poster says dead or alive—she'd prefer dead. While on the trail, she gains the unwanted help of a marshal-turned-bounty hunter intent on catching the killer and bedding her.

In pursuit of the renegade, Jack and Tessa Jane have to deal with the harshness of the Wild West and with their shared desires. However, can a handsome man with secrets and a beautiful woman with a violent past overcome their stubborn ways to share everlasting love? Or will an outlaw destroy them by revealing all their secrets?

When she bargained with the devil of her dreams, they both found their heart's delight.

Lord Demon's Delight

© 2007 Gia Dawn

Lady Jessaline Nolan is as stubborn as her fiery red hair implies; thwarting her father's wishes every chance she gets. The day of her impending forced marriage proves no exception. She swears she would rather marry a Demon of Dunmore than the man her father has chosen.

Lord Llewellyn Dunmore is happily unwed, as the men in his lineage have remained for generations. It's become a family tradition. But he is drawn to the beautiful damsel in distress and agrees to save her on one condition—that she willingly succumb to his every sensual demand. To his utter surprise, she agrees.

While Jessaline's father schemes to bring her back by any means necessary, Jessaline and Llewellyn spend their nights in decadent delight and three rather cranky fairy-godmothers lend their magical help to the lovers.

Darker secrets lurk, however, as well as a shadowy past that Jessaline is unaware of. Can the new love between Jessaline and Llewellyn survive when confronted with hidden truths?

First book in the Demons of Dunmore Series

Available now in ebook and print from Samhain Publishing.